Better *than* Life

MARGARET GUNNING

NEWEST PRESS

National Library of Canada Cataloguing in Publication Data
Gunning, Margaret, 1954-
Better than life / Margaret Gunning.

ISBN 1-896300-69-3

I. Title.
PS8563.U5754B47 2003   C813'.6   C2003-910945-3

Editor: Caterina Edwards
Cover and interior design: Ruth Linka
Cover images: www.mikesteinhauer.com
Author photograph: David Middleton

Excerpts from *The Prophet* by Kahlil Gibran, copyright 1923 by Kahlil Gibran and renewed 1951 by Administrators C.T.A. of Kahlil Gibran Estate and Mary. G. Gibran. Used by permission of Alfred A. Knopf, a division of Random House, Inc.

NeWest Press acknowledges the support of the Canada Council for the Arts and the Alberta Foundation for the Arts, and the Edmonton Arts Council for our publishing program. We also acknowledge the financial support of the Government of Canada through the Book Publishing Industry Development Program (BPIDP) for our publishing activities.

NeWest Press
201–8540–109 Street
Edmonton, Alberta T6G 1E6
(780) 432-9427
www.newestpress.com

1 2 3 4 5 06 05 04 03

NeWest Press is committed to protecting the environment and to the responsible use of natural resources. This book is printed on 100% post-consumer recycled and ancient forest-friendly paper. For more information please visit www.oldgrowthfree.com.

PRINTED AND BOUND IN CANADA

To the memory of Aubrey Melville Smith

"Because your steadfast love is better than life,
my lips will praise you.
So I will bless you as long as I live;
I will lift up my hands and call on your name."

—Psalm 63

Prologue: B U C K

The dog hadn't moved for the past thirty years.

That's a long time to sit still. But then Buck had always been a good and faithful companion, a loyal friend. Or so Whit used to say: old Uncle Whit, gnarled as a stick, his mind as twisted as his body, feeling his way along the walls, nearly blind, mostly deaf, and irretrievably crazy.

Aubrey sat in the rocker with the crushed-velvet seat, once plush and now bald as an old doll, brooding about Uncle Whit. His mother's brother, with that hooded, pointy-eyed look, the look of the Pedlows that jabbed you right to the quick.

Whit had loved Buck as he had never loved another human being. So much so that when his companion died back in 1938, Whit couldn't bear to just bury him in the backyard with the tomato plants. The sight of him still sitting there, his noble spaniel head alertly cocked, always gave strangers the creeps.

Maybe it was the fact that Buck's eyes stared a little too brightly for comfort. The taxidermist had gone a wee bit far in trying to make his subject "lifelike" and had given the old mutt the most crazed look, almost hydrophobic.

Mad dogs and Irishmen, Aubrey thought.

The rocker was a pain in the ass, worn flat on the bottom from the weird obsessive Connar style of rocking perfected by Min. She'd sit there for days on end, knitting big shapeless things out of fine beige wool. Right next to the chair, smelling musty as old Buck himself, was the big dome-shaped radio that Melville Connar had brought home in the deeps of the Depression, the brownish T. Eaton's sticker still on the back. "Such a waste!" Min had exclaimed. Spending thirteen dollars for mere entertainment.

Over the years the grey woven fabric covering the small round speaker had become saturated by the stink of Aubrey's Muriels. He liked to sit there and smoke. Min called it "doing nothing," but it gave him a chance to turn things over in his mind.

Aubrey thought of Melville Connar, and Uncle Whit, and all of his dead kin sunk six feet deep in the Harman cemetery, and because his mind worked in the strange dark way of the Connar mind, he wondered what they looked like now. Anything left at all? Just dust, or were there still some bones? Rags of clothing?

Buck was better-preserved, if a bit threadbare. "That thing has fleas!" Min would bellow, swiping at Buck's stiff carcass with her stick. But Aubrey knew better. Fleas needed blood to survive.

And incidentally, not much in the way of fleas would ever survive on Min Connar these days, desiccated as she was, her shrivelled breasts fallen down to her navel. Well, someone had to help her take a bath these days, and since Mrs. Barham went barmy, it all too often fell on Aubrey. Unlike Buck and the radio, this particular antique had a pulse, and a mouth to match. At least the radio had an on-off switch. But not Min, who could talk the hind leg off a frog in that stage-Irish voice of hers.

She'd gone to bed now, thank God, and he could hear in the next room the roar and rattle of her snoring, a sound almost prehistoric in the midnight stillness of the house. The hockey game was long over and the black-and-white television set in the corner turned off. Buck stared in his eternally faithful way. It was finally time, a time Aubrey could call his own. His mind began to soften and fade backwards, deep into the past. He reached out his hand and clicked the dial on the radio. There was a hiss and a crackle, then the sound of a sprightly jingle sung by a chorus of women in close harmony:

"Pepsi-Cola hits the spot!
Twelve full ounces, that's a lot.
Twice as much for a nickel, too,
Pepsi-Cola is the drink for you!"

1.

Min Connar died several times that year. The first time she died, on a mild April morning in 1968, it threw a bit of a curve at Aubrey. The breakfast tray sat untouched by her bedroom door for ever so long, the tea getting a skin on it, her favourite Pep flakes turning to something resembling wood pulp in the bowl. Min was always up by 8:30 on the dot, but by the time Aubrey had finished reading the Harman Standard at a quarter after ten, the tray was still sitting there, a few fruit flies hovering around the bad banana she insisted he include with her cereal ("There's more flavour to them once they've gone black." "Yes, Min." "Now don't you go giving me those terrible green ones." "No, Min." "Too much snap to 'em. I like my bananas soft." "Anything you say, Min." "And don't be so impertinent. Pretending to agree with me. I know what you're really thinking. And don't call me Min.")

He tapped on the door. She didn't like Aubrey coming into her room even at the best of times. What if she were standing there naked? He pictured her long bluish-grey hair bursting out of its bun, snaking its kinked, untidy way down the length of her caved-in body like an obscene parody of Lady Godiva, and winced at the thought.

But hadn't he helped her in and out of the claw-footed,

brown-streaked tub more times than he cared to remember? Though she'd always insisted he keep his eyes closed: "Don't peek!" "Min, I won't peek. I have a weak stomach, remember?"

Tapped a little louder. No response. Not even her famous wall-shaking snore. Tried the doorknob. Locked. Oh, Min, Min. Can't bear to leave the door open even to your own son? Went into the kitchen to find the skeleton key behind the green glass jar full of the square brown oatcakes that reminded Aubrey of roofing tiles. (Even at eighty-nine, Min still baked on occasion, using ancient Irish recipes as brown and crumbling as the oatcakes themselves.) Fumbled the bedroom door open and stopped short. Something wasn't right. There lay Min with her snaky hair nicely arranged on the pillow around her face. Wearing her new nightie from the Metropolitan, pink floral print with a little bow, still free of pee-stains and food-spills. Ancient as she was, there was something of the young girl about the sweet composure in her face.

Aubrey realized he couldn't hear the little nose-wheeze that indicated she was still breathing. Grabbed the long-handled, silver-backed mirror, the one Cousin Norah sent over from Portadown when Min got married in 1900, and held it under her nose.

Nothing. No fog, no moisture, no trace of living.

"Merciful Jesus." Aubrey was shocked and deeply shamed by the surge of relief he felt in his solar plexus. Knew he should do something, not just stand there like a halfwit.

Well, what do you do when somebody dies? What's the proper response? Isn't there some sort of certificate or something? Bliss. That's it. He'll take care of it. He and

Min liked to trade obscene flirtations during his interminable house calls, even though by now withered old Doc Bliss must have a penis like a stick of pepperoni.

"Dr. Bliss. Connar here. No, not Conner Bryan. Aubrey Connar. You'd better come over right away. Min is . . ." (What should he say? "Stiff"?) "She's in a bad way. You'd better hurry."

For the next twenty minutes he sat on the edge of the bed, waiting for Bliss. Not a stir of life in Min's dry old body. When the doorbell rang he ran to the dim front hall which always seemed to smell faintly of wool coats and pumpkin pie. The two exchanged curt greetings and strode single file into the bedroom.

"Well, Min. Tut tut tut tut tut. This won't do at all."

"Dr. Bliss," Aubrey gasped. "Min's . . ."

"Better get the brandy bottle, Aub."

At that, Min cracked a marbly green eye. Aubrey had never noticed before how much she resembled a desert reptile. A Gila monster, maybe. Jerked herself up to a remarkably erect sitting position for one whose spine curves like a dry wishbone.

"Carman. I want to change my will."

"Oh, Min. For heaven's sake. A little snort will fix you up. Aubrey's gone to get it now." (Indeed, he had fled the room, suddenly overtaken with a fit of coughing.)

"Call Dan Ryerson. I want to cut this ungrateful son of mine out of my will."

"Min, be reasonable."

"I am being reasonable. I'm giving it all to my grandchildren. Eileen's brood—how many of them does she have? Sixteen?"

"I think it's eleven, dear. Here's Aubrey with the

hooch. Now, you just take a sip of this, Min, and—"

Min swiped the glass out of Aubrey's hand and tossed the brandy back in one huge, open-mouthed gulp.

"Call Dan Ryerson *now.*"

"Min, let me listen to your heart." Dr. Bliss warmed the bell of the stethoscope in his hand, not wanting to chill the old buzzard so soon after her "crisis." Min looked drunk. Her greenish eyes rolled upward in a grotesque parody of flirtation. Vivien Leigh trying to seduce Ashley Wilkes in *Gone with the Wind.*

"Are you going to be naughty, Carman?" Min's eyes gleamed in anticipation of the doctor's warm hands fumbling with the front of her fresh new nightie from the Metropolitan. Aubrey noticed a humming in his ears, faint at first, then louder.

He fled from the room, then out the front door, finding it almost impossible to breathe. Stood taking gulps of air on the slightly sagging, white-painted front porch. Neighbourhood children thought there was something strange or special about this house because one of the bricks by the front door had a cat's-paw imprint on it. And of course they'd heard rumours that there was a dead dog in there that used to belong to a crazy old man. To Aubrey, the house was nondescript, just the place he had lived in for all of his fifty-four years, so much like every other little old brick house in Harman that he could think of nothing that set it apart.

Except its location. It was right next door to the Belgian bakery, which served as a nerve centre for the entire town of Harman. Aubrey had a sudden, overwhelming urge for a cup of coffee and one of Guillaume's potato-flour doughnuts. Having caught his breath, he headed down the street, dodging a pack of whooping teenagers in bell-bottomed jeans and garish T-shirts. *Hippies,* Aubrey thought. *Shouldn't they be in school?* Until the past year or so, these same young people were getting good grades, going bowling on weekends, obeying their elders.

Aubrey heaved the door of the bakery open, noticing with annoyance the ancient, dusty wedding cake in the front window with its calcified bride and groom.

"Guillaume. How are you, my good man."

"Aubrey. How is Min?"

"Took a spell this morning. Had to call Dr. Bliss again." He made a face. "Coffee and a spudnut, Guy."

Guillaume served up a long, narrow doughnut glazed with gleaming cerise icing, and a white mug of coffee strong enough to stick your teeth together. Aubrey ambled over to one of the round, gold-flecked Formica tables. A mother and her two young children sat nearby. The kiddies whining, of course. Snot running down their faces. Aubrey thought: this is almost as bad as putting up with Min. And then the bakery door jangled again.

Worse and worse. It was Dot. The whiff told you before you even saw her. Armpits and stale burlap. The young mother grabbed her son's grubby hand and pulled her daughter protectively closer.

Dot was in full regalia with all her bags and tatters. She shuffled up to the counter and began to count out pennies from an ancient woven change purse. Probably found it in somebody's garbage. Every town had to have a Dot, Aubrey guessed. But this one made you more uncomfortable than most.

"Coffee, Guy."

"Of course, Dot. Ten cents."

"Any day-olds?"

"I'll check in the back." There was a sort of understanding that Guy would save her all the superfluous items, the lopsided eclairs and broken cookies, the cake marked "Happy 90th Birthday Bernie" that no one ever collected because Bernie suddenly dropped dead of a heart attack, the witch's fingers that no longer sold as of the first of November. Guy came back with a paper bag of kaiser rolls that had probably been sitting there for a week.

Dot's arm shot out and she grabbed the bag of buns the same way Min had snatched the brandy out of Aubrey's hand. It reminded him of a *National Geographic* special he'd seen in which the slow-motion camera caught the lightning-fast snaking-out of a chameleon's tongue, a frighteningly precise snatch-and-grab. Dot shuffled over to a table near the two little children, who were now asking embarrassing questions of their mother.

"Mummie, why is that lady wearing so many sweaters?"

"Shhhhh, Denise, that's not polite."

"Mummie . . . what's in that bag? It's moving."

And indeed, one of Dot's multitude of holey jute bags did seem to have a life of its own. The sides of it were seething as if she had a snake tunnelling around in there. Maybe one of her cats, Aubrey thought. No one even knew how many cats Dot had, and it was understood around Harman that an unwanted cat could be left on her doorstep. "More than three cats," Guillaume often opined, "is a sickness," and Aubrey tended to agree.

Then a small, rat-like head appeared at the top of the bag. Little Denise let out a scream.

"S'okay," Dot slurred. "It's just my chinchilla."

"Chinchillas, Dot!" Guy cried. "Are you raising them for profit, then?"

"I have two," Dot said in a gruff sort of way, as if to discourage further questioning on her latest enterprise.

"Where's the other one?" the little boy said. His mother shushed him, too late.

"Can't find him. I don't have any cages yet. This is the female. Can't leave her alone in the house—might scare the cats." She pushed the rat-head down into the unspeakable clutter of broken stuff in the bag. The sides heaved for a moment, then fell still. Probably asphyxiated, Aubrey thought, by the fumes of all of Dot's rotten old junk.

"How's Min?" Dot fumbled around in the pockets of her fringy sweaters for a cigarette.

"Took a bad spell. Doc Bliss is with her now."

"Well, at her age." Dot coughed raucously, then spat a wad of phlegm into her yellowed handkerchief. Aubrey was surprised it wasn't the floor. Putting on manners for the kiddies, he guessed.

"So, Aub. You won't be coming into that fortune for a while yet, then." Dot could really shock you. She wasn't nearly so slow as she seemed, and when there was money involved, she was sharp as a chest pain.

"Now, Dot. Don't believe the rumours. Mother's been a widow for a long time. Surely Dad's money is all used up by now."

"Used up, my kneecap," Dot wheezed, sucking on her lit Camel. "Everybody in Harman knows she's sittin' on a bloody fortune. Keeps it in a mattress in the attic."

"Dot, that's nonsense. There's no mattress."

"Eileen'll be after it," Dot declared. "How many kids does she have? Sixteen?"

"Eleven, Dot."

"And all by different husbands?"

"There were only five."

"And what about . . . what's their names anyway? The twins?"

"I haven't seen 'em in fifteen years."

"Shame on you, Aubrey. Blood is thicker than water," followed by a gale of coughing. Strange for her to say this since as far as anyone in Harman knew, Dot had neither kith nor kin, nor chick nor child, anywhere in this wide world. "What was that feud about, anyway? Property?"

"The Connars don't have any."

"A woman?"

"It was a question of honour." Aubrey didn't want to talk about his estrangement from his brothers. Half the Connar clan wasn't speaking to the other half anyway. Everyone in town knew that, and took delight in commenting on it. You'd think they were worlds away from Aubrey and Min, but most of them lived somewhere around Horgansville, less than an hour's drive from Harman, and didn't Aubrey sometimes drive all the way into Toronto with his girlfriend Pearl just to go hear that Jon Vickers fellow shout his lungs out at the opera? That was the way people thought. The good folk of Harman excelled at disapproval.

Then, thank God, the bell jangled again, relieving the knot of discomfort in Aubrey's gut. Doc Bliss strode in, beaming. "Aub! Don't worry. She's out like a light. Left her sleeping like the dead, if you'll pardon the expression. That's pretty good stuff you got there. Hello, Dot."

"Carman." What was it about her tone, that little curved inflection in her voice? Decaying remnants of seduction. It gave Aubrey the creeps.

"Guess I'd better get back," he mumbled.

"Aub. *Sit down.* Enjoy your coffee. Do you want me writing prescriptions for you next? For your nerves?" Dr. Bliss pulled up a chair right next to Dot, who was smiling enigmatically, as if she'd won some small victory.

"But Mrs. Barham can't come in for a month."

"Mrs. Barham had a nervous breakdown, Aubrey, and do you know why? She ran to Min's beck and call, that's why. Mrs. Barham, get me some licorice allsorts. Mrs. Barham, there's a funny smell in the bathroom. Why haven't you cleaned it? Mrs. Barham, these are the wrong digestive biscuits. And so on, and so on. Now I see it happening to you, and it concerns me." Dr. Bliss raked a hand over his nearly bald pink skull, slicking down his stringy black comb-over. Dot blew out her cigarette smoke a la Bette Davis, in a gesture that probably went back thirty years. The bag at her feet heaved and Dot kicked it.

"What've you got in there, Dot? A rattlesnake?"

"Cobra," she said, narrowing her eyes. Come to think of it, her eyes *were* a touch exotic, like a photo Aubrey had once seen of Emily Carr. He felt a strange stirring and quickly squashed it as Dot stubbed out her cigarette.

"So how's that sister of yours, Aubrey?" Everyone in Harman seemed to think Eileen was much more interesting than Aubrey. All those husbands, he guessed, while Aubrey had stubbornly remained unmarried. Yes, he had Pearl, an open secret, but that wasn't the same. Nearly twenty years with the same girlfriend was too predictable, even though they did dare to travel together as Mr. and Mrs. Smith.

"Having trouble with the kids."

"How many—"

"Eleven. So one of them is bound to be in trouble at any given time."

"Wasn't one of them—you know, the youngest girl, the teenager—"

"Pregnant?"

"Well, I wouldn't quite put it that way."

"How would you, then? You're a doctor. 'Knocked up?'"

"Aubrey. You're getting irritable. You'd benefit from the Librium, you know."

"Pills. And a brandy chaser, then. Is that what you want?"

"Of course not, Aubrey. We know you only keep it in the house for Min."

"Is that what people say? Why does it even come up?"

"It doesn't, Aubrey. Everyone thinks of you as a model citizen now, believe me."

"Except I still keep it in the house. For Min." Aubrey was surprised at the rawness of his nerves. Maybe he did need a break. Suddenly Dot put her veiny old hand on his forearm. A subversive thrill jolted through his whole body and went right to the spot. He had forgotten how he used to drink with Dot. A murk of memory stirred, an unbearable mixture of pleasure and despair.

"I've got to get back," he gasped, and clanged out the door.

A moment later Dr. Bliss turned to look at Dot with a little furrow of professional concern in his brow.

"D'you really think he's on the wagon?"

2.

The next time Min died, Aubrey was prepared for it. She'd had Dan Ryerson over for the longest time, plying him with so much strong black Irish tea and so many digestive biscuits that he could barely walk. Aubrey heard him afterwards in the bathroom, pissing his brains out. Min's tea was lethal.

So when he heard a horrendous prolonged thundering and crashing behind the cellar door, followed by a protracted piercing wail, he wasn't even particularly surprised. Just Min at her favourite sport again. Might as well go along with it. He raced down the cellar steps crying, "Mother! Mother! My God, what have you done?"

Min had arranged herself artfully at the bottom of the stairs, limbs twisted, her body inert. She seemed to have mastered the art of not breathing, and to his shock Aubrey found that he couldn't even detect a pulse. Maybe she had gained complete mastery over all of her bodily functions like those Indian yogis Aubrey used to read about. It wouldn't surprise him.

"Mother. Speak to me." This was like a vaudeville routine, but at least Aubrey knew his part, as if it had all been rehearsed in advance.

No response. Then he saw something in the corner

of his eye—a big, dented aluminum trash barrel which she'd probably kicked down the stairs to create the proper theatrical crash-and-bang effect. Well, it sure sounded like Min's old bones, which had probably turned to aluminum by now anyway, or whatever old bones turn to when they rust with age.

"Mother. Don't leave us now. Hang on. I'll get you some brandy. I'll call Dr. Bliss."

The name provoked a flicker of response in one blue-veined eyelid. The old reptile. Still lusting after Carman after all these years. Aubrey went over to the utility sink and turned on the tap, wetting his hands. He flicked his fingers in Min's face. Yes, a definite twitch. This corpse had good reflexes.

A long, keening Irish moan issued up from Min's concave chest.

"All you care about is the money."

"Nonsense! Mother, how can you say that?"

"Talk to Eileen, Aubrey. Talk to her. Before it's too late."

"Mother, Eileen and I have nothing to say to each other. She's busy with her family anyway."

"How many—"

"Twenty-seven. At last count."

"Aubrey, don't be impertinent with me. And what about Barlow and Dwight?"

"My God, Min. Not that again."

"I told you not to call me that. You try to act as if you have no brothers and sisters." Min sat up abruptly, and Aubrey was shocked at the sudden strength in her. Spry as a sparrow, in spite of her twisty old bones. "You know what people are saying."

"What are they saying, Mother?"

"That you're driving a wedge between me and the rest of my children. Not to mention all those grandchildren. And you're only doing it to keep your place in my will. Well, I've changed it so you might as well stop this. Acting as if you're some sort of only child. And you're not even the oldest."

No, that would be Eileen. Eileen, six foot two, with a chest like a pouter pigeon and a personality like an express train. The bossy big sister. She had first-born written all over her. While Aubrey was stuck with the chronic confusion of being a youngest. Weren't they supposed to be irresponsible? So where was Eileen when Min peed her bed again and had to be changed? Where were Barlow and Dwight when—*oh for the Lord's sake, I've got to stop thinking like this.*

"Aubrey," Min wheezed. "Help me get up."

"If you didn't pull these stunts all the time I wouldn't have to be helping you up, Mother."

"So you're just going to let me lie here and rot."

"Of course not, Mother. Lying down, playing dead, and getting up again keeps you in trim. It's sort of like calisthenics."

Min pressed her lips together sourly to keep from smiling, but Aubrey saw the telltale flash of amusement in her eyes. He scooped her up off the damp black floor—she could've broken or at least bruised something, even without falling down the bloody stairs—and carried her up the steep flight to the back hall.

"Oh Aubrey," she sighed, rolling her eyes, "a mother couldn't ask for a better son."

"That's not what you were saying a minute ago."

"Wisha. That's gone."

It drove Aubrey crazy, the way she wouldn't let him hate her.

No sooner had he settled her in her bed with a good, stiff snort of brandy than the telephone rang. Aubrey groaned inwardly. It was probably that drunken old bat again, the female baritone with a voice like ten miles of bad road, asking for "Gunther." Aubrey kept telling her she had the wrong number. Still she called. "Gunther. *Gunther.*" Aubrey couldn't think of a single Gunther in all the town of Harman. Sometimes when she was really plastered, she sang. "Rose of Tralee." *Too-ra-loo-ra-loo-ral.* Once Aubrey grabbed the phone and before she could utter a single syllable, he let fly with his best Sunday-morning tenor: "Oh Danny Boy, you've got the wro-ong nu-umber . . ." It turned out to be the Reverend Ninian Sanderson wanting to pay Min a pastoral visit. Took Aubrey a lot of explaining to convince old Nin that he was sober.

The phone rang twice, three times. Oh, for God's sake. Gunther's not here. He picked up the receiver reluctantly. "You have the wrong nu—"

"Aubrey?"

"Yes."

"Don't you know who this is?"

Aubrey went blank.

"Am I supposed to know?"

"Aubrey. Your own sister."

"*Eileen?*"

"Has it come to this, then? That you don't even know your own blood kin?"

"It's just that . . . Eileen, it's . . . it's just that you never call."

"Never call! Never call! Did it ever occur to you that these telephone lines work both ways?"

"I'm sorry, Eileen. What was it you wanted?"

"Wanted? Why would I want anything from you or from anyone else? What a suspicious mind you have, Aubrey Connar. Don't you trust anyone?"

"It's been a long time, Eileen. I guess you could say that I'm out of practice."

On the other end of the line, he felt her smile.

"How's Mother?" At last, Eileen was asking after Min, for the first time in how many years? Yes, there was always a Christmas card, and even a bit of money once in a while. The odd letter from her was so full of horror—all the latest disasters with her huge brood and their bad marriages and failed jobs and wayward children—that Aubrey recoiled from them, rushing through the details to get to the cheque.

"Well enough. Took a bit of a spell this morning."

"A spell?" Eileen made it sound like something cast by a coven of witches.

"It's nothing serious. She's eighty-nine."

"Aubrey, she really should be in a home."

"She'd be dead in a month, Eileen, and you know it."

"It's unnatural, the two of you living together in that awful old house."

"If I didn't, who would look after her?"

"You use her as an excuse."

"An excuse?"

"To stay the same. To never get married. To keep the same job for fifteen years."

"Eileen."

"I'm just trying to help you."

"Like always."

"Yes, like always."

"So should I model my life after yours, then? Is that what you want?"

"Oh, Christ." She took a breath, tried to recover herself. "Aubrey. We're blood kin, and Mother won't last much longer. Doesn't that mean anything to you?"

A silence.

"It does, Eileen."

"Can we make peace, then?"

"Maybe." He fumbled around in his plaid shirt pocket for a cigar. The conversation was sucking the life out of him.

"I'm coming over to see her next week," Eileen announced, and Aubrey dropped his lit Muriel on the diamond-patterned carpet like a live coal.

"Coming over . . . shouldn't she be warned?" He immediately regretted his choice of words.

"Warned!" Fortunately, Eileen burst out laughing. "What am I, a plague?"

"That's not what I meant."

"The hell it isn't."

"I only meant I should . . . prepare her. She hasn't seen you in . . . when was the last time she saw you?"

"Wednesday," Eileen said briskly. "I'll be there Wednesday at ten o'clock in the morning. It'll take me about half an hour from Horgansville, so I'll have to leave by, let's see . . ."

'That's an hour's drive, Eileen."

"An *hour?*" she snorted. "Sure, the way *you* drive." Aubrey pictured her at the wheel and winced. Any time he'd been a passenger, he'd had to hold on to his seat, close his eyes, and pray.

"I'll be at work," Aubrey protested.

"Don't you trust me to see her alone?"

"It's just that . . . "

"Take an hour off, then. Soapy will understand."

Sure. Soapy Hudson knew that Aubrey's whole existence revolved around Min. He also knew Eileen. Knew her in the Biblical sense; he'd been married to her once, right before Dermot Smith and after Rodney McGraw.

"Just don't drive too fast."

"You're such a good brother, Aubrey."

"I just don't want you to go piling into a tree."

"Give my love to Mother, then. *Mwah.*" The air-kiss was her way of signing off, modelled after Dinah Shore.

Aubrey hung up. Suddenly he had a tremendous urge for chicken. Min was sick of it, that much he knew, but it made him want it even more.

It was an enormous thrill to the good people of Harman when in the summer of 1967 a Kentucky Fried Chicken opened on Tamarack Drive. It was the year of the Centennial, men were sprouting sideburns and moustaches, and there was an air of festivity everywhere. Having a Kentucky Fried Chicken meant that Harman was *somewhere,* not just some two-bit tobacco town with one movie theatre, a library with twenty-eight books in it, and no sense of the finer things. Since Aubrey loathed cooking and Min couldn't stand up for long enough to do very much in the kitchen, the Colonel's grease-saturated, mouth-puckeringly salty chicken became a staple.

"Cabbage salad," Min would say as Aubrey headed out the door to pick up an order.

"It's called coleslaw, Mother."

"Cabbage salad. Get the family size. And a big carton of gravy."

Min barely touched the chicken, eating only the frizzled, paprika-tinged skin. But cabbage salad she could eat in obscene quantities. Mint-green, pulverized beyond recognition, laced with something that must have been horseradish, it bore no relation to any cabbage that ever lived, and Min shovelled it in by the heaped forkful, not even needing to chew.

Sometimes the Colonel would appear on the television to flog his product, and Min would point her finger at the screen and say, "There he is. Colonel Saunders." She always pronounced it that way, no matter how many times she was corrected. To Min, Harland Sanders was the perfect Southern gentleman. He was like a character out of a book, *Gone with the Wind* maybe, legendary. Aubrey hated to break it to her that he was just some short-order cook who made good, and whose only claim to Colonelhood was that phony white suit and string tie.

"Bless his heart," she would murmur, getting a little misty. Only Min Connar would be soft-headed enough to cry at a chicken commercial.

But she took great comfort in his presence. It was reassuring. The TV could be unsettling, these days. For one thing, her beloved Ed Sullivan Show had been completely taken over. Last Sunday Ed announced "something for all you youngsters"—a violently discordant rock 'n' roll group called—what was it now, something about a President— Jefferson—Jefferson something. "Feed your head!" screamed the female lead singer. (Imagine a woman doing such a thing.) "Feed your head!" What was that supposed to mean? Where was Jimmy Durante when she needed him most?

Aubrey walked the seven blocks to the Harman Chicken Villa in the rain, trying to clear his head. So Eileen was coming over next Wednesday. Aubrey wasn't even sure what she looked like now. What was she—fifty-eight?

Pushing sixty, with children from fifteen to thirty-six, and who knows how many grandkids. She was offhand about them, counting them off on her fingers, then giving up at a certain point. She must have gone greyer and gotten stouter, but she'd still tower over everyone else—the legendary Connar stature, coming out more in the women than the men.

The rapidly revolving bucket with the picture of Colonel Sanders on it hove into view, and with it came a strong odour of burnt grease. Aubrey began to salivate like a conditioned dog. As he heaved the door open, he caught sight of something. Or someone. Around the back of the restaurant, somebody was rummaging through a garbage can. A nondescript figure in saggy damp clothing. No, no, not Dot. He shook his head, let go of the door, and walked around the back.

"Dot, for God's sake. Here, here's fi' dollars, buy yourself some chicken."

"I couldn't, Aubrey. There's plenty of food here." She showed him a nearly complete dinner in a box that someone had thrown away. It was shocking, Aubrey thought, wasting food like that, a sin. But the look in Dot's eyes indicated that it wouldn't be wasted.

"Suit yourself, then, Dot."

"The cats eat the bones."

"Not good for them."

"Not good for *you* either, my dear." She shot him a glance with those uncanny grey eyes. "Say hello to Eileen for me, will you?"

Aubrey stared. *How on earth did she . . .* With great dignity she shoved her dinner into a burlap sack and began the long, wet trudge home.

3.

 Eileen remembered the first time.

It was hard to believe. And unlikely. Her big, solid, fifty-eight-year-old body had been buffeted about by so many men over the years, some of them so inept in bed that it was a wonder they found their way in at all. They grunted and heaved, the fat ones especially, with a comical look on their faces, about as intelligent as spawning salmon willing to smash their own skulls in if necessary to ring the gong of reproduction.

But it had been different once, and even if Eileen's mind fought to obscure the knowledge because it made the present seem so unbearable, her body remembered.

Her body remembered being twenty-one, very tall and strong, with a firm, good figure. A strapping, athletic girl with magnificent large breasts that stood straight out without a hint of a sag. And a virgin. In those days, nobody even used words like that. Chastity was a given, with only the worst women allowing themselves to be besmirched.

Eileen did not begin to menstruate until she was fifteen, and she knew virtually nothing of how it was between a man and a woman because nobody would tell her anything. Her entire sex education had come from watching films starring Greta Garbo and John Gilbert. Things were just different then. Girlhood was preserved for years longer, with wholesome magazines devoted to the girl's life and shapeless clothing designed to hide the burgeoning contours of a sexually ripening body. It was only in the movies that women wore form-fitting dresses, women like Jean Harlow, who had something decidedly wicked about her, or Clara Bow, the "It Girl," who even dared to show her knees.

Eileen was not prepared for the shock of Shelton Gramercy. Was it his age? The fact that he was divorced? How many women had he had in his life, and how had he managed to unlock the secrets of their bodies? Subsequent experiences in the boudoir horrified Eileen, because after Shelton, she assumed all men would know about the refined art of bodily pleasure. It was a shock to realize that hardly anyone did.

It was no wonder he felt attracted to Eileen Connar. There was a freshness about her, an uncomplicated, unspoiled quality that provided a counterpoint to his own tangled, brooding writer's soul. She was a shopgirl at Carmody's Dry Goods, plain and simple, reminding him of the "million dollar baby in the five-and-ten-cent store" of popular song.

And Gramercy's conscience never bothered him about the difference in age. Charlie Chaplin took young women under his wing and initiated them into the pleasures of the flesh, didn't he, so wasn't he actually doing her a favour? Gramercy cut quite a figure in those days. He was divorced, which automatically made him something of an exotic in Harman. And he had actually written a book, a real book that appeared in the stores, called *Edge of Sin*, exposing the seething underbelly of a seemingly wholesome small town. Everyone in Harman hated this book with a passion, and everyone in Harman bought a copy and read it cover to cover, feverishly searching for themselves somewhere in the story.

At least Gramercy had a proper job with an insurance company, so he didn't go around calling himself a writer, which in Harman would have been considered the height of lunacy. But his authorly status did lend him a certain cachet. He was not very tall but handsome in the manner of Ronald Coleman, with a pencil moustache and a borzoi he walked on a leash. There were murmurings among the townsfolk that he drank too much, but wasn't that other writer fellow, what's his name now anyways, that F. Scott Fitzgerald, wasn't he a bit of a drinker too? Maybe they can't help it, these writers, with their heads crammed full of such beautiful nonsense.

Others were not so willing to cut him this much slack. "I knew him when he was still called Percy Gribble and working at Dan Hudson's lumberyard for fifty cents a day." But to Eileen he was a shining figure, head and shoulders above anyone else in Harman. When his lips lightly brushed her earlobe, it set her entire being adazzle with desire. His caresses turned her spine to water, creating incomprehensible eruptive sensations in her lower body that almost frightened her. The word orgasm was not even remotely in anyone's vocabulary in Harman in those days, so Eileen assumed she had invented the phenomenon herself.

They met in secret. If the affair had been out in the open, it wouldn't have lasted more than a week. And much as Shelton Gramercy loved Eileen, he wasn't too sure he wanted to be seen in public with her. In public he preferred the company of chic divorcees in their thirties with long cigarette holders and smart little round hats with veils, women that from a distance could pass for Dorothy Parker. Never mind that there were all of two of them in Harman; that's what he preferred. So he and Eileen met furtively in cheap hotel rooms late at night. (Eileen had become adept at crawling out of windows; if Mother had known, she would have had a fit, as if there had never been any passion in her own life.) It took some getting used to, the water-stained wallpaper, the sway-backed mattress and stale, urinous smell, but once he began to touch her body, it was so lovely that she quickly forgot about the pissy, distasteful surroundings.

It's a story as old as Adam and Eve: the fresh young girl, the sophisticated older man, the reassurances *I won't put it in all the way; It can't happen the first time; Don't worry, I'll pull it out before I, you know*. For each and every girl this happens to, it is happening for the first time, and it is for all the world as if it is for the only time in human history. Some sort of magic would protect her from getting in trouble, especially if she didn't think about it very much.

Four months into the pregnancy, Mother blew the whistle. At first she tried to dismiss the retching in the toilet every morning, telling herself it was just the girl's nerves, or something that ran in her blood. (Hadn't Min's own father died of indigestion at the age of forty-eight?) But when Eileen's neat work uniform began to strain across the stomach, a deep alarm sounded in her mind, an ancient knowledge telling her that her firstborn was in a bad way.

"Eileen. Turn around, girl! Don't hump your shoulders."

"I'm not humping them, Mother."

"Stand up straight. Merciful God, girl. How far gone are you?"

"Mother!"

"Don't try to fool me. D'ye think I don't know about these things? I've had four babes of my own, my dear, and let me tell you, they go in a lot easier than they come out."

"It's just that I'm fat, Mother, from all the chocolate cherries at Carmody's. We get them for free."

"Fat, is it. This is a nine-month fatness. So who is he? A boy at work?"

"Just . . . someone."

"Aha, someone. So now we know it isn't a box of chocolates. Does he have a name?"

"I can't tell you."

Min's eyes pierced Eileen. "Are you protecting his name, or are you ashamed of him?"

"The . . . first one."

"Married?"

"No!"

"Older?"

"A little."

"Such as, twenty-some years?"

Eileen squirmed.

"I don't suppose he'd consider marrying you."

Even Eileen, playing Eve to Shelton's Adam in their own personal Eden, wasn't that naive. Her lower lip began to tremble.

"Eileen. Listen to me, girl. You can let your shoulders down now; this isn't an inspection. I want you to think. Are there any boys you like? Boys your own age, I mean."

Eileen thought of fish-faced Frankie McAdam and

Bruce Knobb with the sour body odour and Russell Mudge with his repugnant, tongue-thrusting kisses, and she began to cry in earnest.

"Have you ever talked to Robbie Davison, now?"

"Mother, you don't mean it."

"Now I want you to think carefully about this, my dear. He's well off and single. From a good family. Churchgoers."

"Mother, he's a nancy boy."

"Don't use expressions like that with me." Min was thinking furiously, her brain whirring so hard it almost made a noise. Hadn't she seen Robbie Davison come out of the men's room at the Caprice Theatre, followed a few moments later by a shamefaced Sean Stanigan, the only other nancy boy in all of Harman?

Min Connar was formulating a plan, and when that happens, God help us all. And so it came to pass that there was a grand wedding at St. Andrew's United Church in the summer of 1931, and all of Harman marvelled at how the nancy boy Robbie Davison finally got married, "so I guess we were wrong about him all along."

And thus began the dire chain of misfortune that was Eileen Connar's marital history. No one needed to know that the nuptials were driven by terror of exposure rather than love, nor that the blessed event that followed five months later had nothing to do with the nancy boy's genetic code.

If people saw a chance resemblance to a certain writer in little Shelby Percival Davison, no one said. No one even noticed the similarity in names (except Min, who rolled her eyes at the christening). Shelton Gramercy, nee Percy Gribble, did the right thing and pretended he didn't know

Eileen when she walked down the streets of Harman with her new baby in a buggy. Eileen absorbed this miserable slight without visibly reacting, demonstrating that almost supernatural female grace and resilience which always goes unsung, even unnoticed. Likewise she endured Robbie's pathetic attempts at lovemaking, his cold hands and coughing fits, his undisguised distaste for her ripe body, the smells and sounds that she couldn't help.

She went through the motions of being a good wife: she cooked and cleaned exactly the way Mother had taught her to, and she was never out of smart hats, Robbie being the new manager of Davison's Millinery, his father's business. They looked well in church on Sunday mornings, the little family of three, though of course poor Eileen couldn't help towering over Robbie, even in flat shoes. The baby was striking to look at, as if he had a movie star for a father and not that poor soul Robbie with the womanish ways. Those who were adept at calculating dates knew such a strapping babe could never have been born after a mere five months in the oven, but in the manner of the times they kept their mouths shut, at least in public.

Ah, Eileen! No matter how bleak things look now, don't ever think you are stuck there for good. She had no way of seeing ahead, or of knowing that she would go on to spring one prison after another. By age fifty she would wear a necklace of names, Eileen Margaret Connar Davison Hale McGraw Hudson Smith, each name a story in itself. A link in a chain or a jewel on a string, it was hard to tell which, because the pleasures and the miseries were so bound up in each other. What was that poem Shelton had taught her? It seemed naughty and it had shocked her.

Crazy Jane Talks with the Bishop. By a great Irish poet, he said, and the gist of it was: "the place we feel all those delights in bed is right next door to where we shit." (Though it's doubtful Yeats would have paraphrased it in quite that way.)

Eileen remembered the way Shelton would lean forward darkly and recite the last verse in those throbbing, actorish tones:

> A woman can be proud and stiff
> When on love intent;
> But Love has pitched his mansion in
> The place of excrement;
> For nothing can be sole or whole
> That has not been rent.

That last bit sailed right past her head, but the other part, about Love pitching his mansion you-know-where, made sense to her because bliss and shit were so impossible to separate—you always got the both of them in one, whether you wanted to or not.

Eileen was learning, learning. Misfortune had given her a crash course. Though she didn't know it at the time, she had a choice to make after Shelton and the pregnancy; she could have gone hard. She could have cultivated bitterness as a way of being for the rest of her natural days. The fact that she didn't spoke for her largeness of heart. But damaged? Of course she was. She'd have years, decades of chaos all tangled in with joy as she careened from man to man, babies flying out of her in all directions.

She should have been the worst mother in the world, but she wasn't. Her children all came out in one piece, so to speak. And each man she married, at least after Robbie, she loved, or thought she did. Certainly she loved the smell of them and the feel of them and the low, heartstopping thrum of their male voices. Secretly she thought it was a sin against God not to love men, their big firm-limbed bodies and whiskery, scratchy faces, the touching lies they half-believed themselves. Men were more potent than whisky, she always thought, and even harder to give up.

"What cannot be cured must be endured" became her motto, her cry. Eileen was no whiner. She kept her head up and her spine straight through all this catastrophe, and walked proud. She wasn't Min Connar's daughter for nothing. Never mind how thin the Irish blood ran in the family today (for Min, though she often lied about it, had been born in Aylmer, not County Down). The blood still thundered and danced and led its people forward into battle. For Eileen the battle was a personal one—a strike for dignity. The fact that she pulled it off was one of those rare and unlikely miracles that no one pays the slightest attention to. It goes unnoticed, like most human magnificence.

So here she was, sailing back into her aging mother's life like a ship all a-billow, wearing her misfortunes proudly, as her warlike kin had taught her. Never surrender—never, no never. Keep your head up, your back straight, and look your enemy bang in the eye. And he might just look back at you with something like respect.

4.

The old radio in the parlour was the closest thing Aubrey Connar had to a best friend.

It was a wonderful deal. Think of it. Having someone who's always there, who doesn't judge, doesn't answer back. Who just *is*. Except for a few dents and a scratch here and there, it looked pretty much the same as when Melville Connar lugged it home all those years ago, and it didn't have that disconcerting habit of changing that everyone else seemed to have.

Aubrey had been a young buck of twenty-four then, full of piss and vinegar and a sense of the future. He remembered how mature he felt, as if he knew everything and could see ahead with great clarity, unlike now, when perplexity and murkiness were the order of the day.

When it was new, the radio had driven Uncle Whit crazy. Not that he had much distance to go. Whit lived upstairs in a small room that reeked of smoke and was cluttered with books and newspapers and old copies of *Argosy* magazine. Leave him alone, and he might be all right. Just one of those strange men that you see sitting in the park, talking to themselves.

But the sprightly dance music and Rudy Vallee songs that poured out of the big domed box would set him to ranting, a great Irish rant that made little sense: "Tools of our destruction! It's a p'isen. Straight from the divil himself. A judgement on all the Connars!" Spit would fly out of his mouth as he worked himself up: "The day of reckoning. Chippies in their scarlet gowns! Dance halls! Perdition!"

"Oh, Whit, just shut up," Min would say with as much patience as she could muster. He'd simmer down eventually, if she made him a nice pot of the barley soup he loved so much. "More," he'd command, downing bowl after bowl, the sweat pouring off him.

Whit had always been around, a presence in the house, as far back as Aubrey could remember, shielded from reality by the family's benevolence. Melville Connar tolerated him, because it was the Christian thing to do, but he didn't like him. For one thing, Whit was a rival male presence in the house, a threat to his paternal authority. On top of that, he frightened the children.

He'd get after Aubrey with that old black shillelagh of his, the one Melville's father, Hamish Connar, had brought over from Portadown all those years ago. He'd rage and thunder about the boy being full of the devil, which was largely true. Buck would go slink under Whit's brass-framed bed with his trembling bottom sticking out from underneath until his master's fit had passed. Min called it "the black rage" and said her brother couldn't help it, 'twas the brain fever when he was a boy. Whit would no more strike a child with a shillelagh than he'd ask a woman to marry him, and everybody knew it. But his threats were good for a thrill of fright.

And afterwards there'd be amends in the form of an empty cigar tube—"Here, boy. To keep your coppers in." (Whit was still doing this after Aubrey's twentieth birthday.)

Sometimes there'd even be money—"Fi' cents." Aubrey had come to realize that giving money made older male relatives feel powerful and lifted their esteem a notch or two in the eyes of the youngsters. It also made their worst behaviour somehow forgivable.

Aubrey sat by the radio, sucking on a Muriel as he did nearly every night of his life, letting the smoke out with a long blue sigh. He settled in for a deep brood, a thick, potent stew of a brood. He was perplexed. When he was perplexed, his brow furrowed, and when his brow furrowed he bore a striking resemblance to his father, dead now for almost thirty years.

Melville Connar passed along most of his genetic traits, both physical and spiritual, to his children and grandchildren, and his presence would likely keep echoing on down the generations into all of eternity. This reminded Aubrey of the magnificent stud horse Justin Morgan, who sired an entire breed that looked just like him. In racing circles, they'd say he "stamped his get."

Aubrey was brooding about get. He held a letter in his hand as he sat in the bare-assed old rocker, puffing and exhaling smoke. It was late—nearly midnight—and tomorrow morning Eileen would arrive for God knows what reason—money, amends, nostalgia? For a splendid opportunity to nag? And now this letter, bringing with it a sick sense of disruption, of murk disturbed. Things had gone along for so long the way they were, on a level, neither good nor bad. But a new seed was cracking open, and God only knew what foul fruit it would ultimately bear.

He thought about fruit, get, offspring. He thought of casual breeding expressions like "throw" and wondered if they would apply in human terms. He thought of consequences. He thought of the past, a seething miasma of darkness and suffering. Aubrey had put the plug in the jug just in time, before his liver blew up and his life imploded, but the years of chaos had left a string of damage.

He'd been good at one thing—escape. After all, he'd practiced so long and hard, he couldn't help but get good at it. It made him ashamed, all the messes he had run away from. Sure, he joked about it, particularly after he got sober. Every Father's Day he'd make gruff comments about all those little bastards running around out there not even knowing who their father was. He'd turn it into a grim jest, how he'd lost track of them all years ago, and good riddance to the little buggers anyway.

And now he held this letter in his hand. He had only read it once, and ever since he had been trembling uncontrollably.

> Dear Mr. Connar,
>
> Not long ago I received a correspondence from my natural mother, Miss Faith Farnsworth, revealing the secret of my birth. I have long suspected that I was adopted, though I had no way of confirming it up to now. For reasons of her own, Miss Farnsworth waited until my twenty-first birthday to reveal the truth to me.
>
> I decided to contact you, Mr. Connar, to see if you have any interest in pursuing a relationship with me, your natural son. I wish to emphasize that this is entirely my own choice; my birth

mother asks nothing of you, either financially or emotionally. Now that I have reached manhood, I need to know more about who my father is. I hope you will be willing to write to me at the address below.

Sincerely,
Robert Douglas Hemphill

Aubrey could not even imagine replying to the letter. What would he say to the boy? That he was sorry he'd made love to Faith Farnsworth all those years ago? In truth he wasn't sorry at all. Mind you, he should have been more careful. French letters were hard to come by in those days—you had to go right up to the pharmacist's counter at the Rexall and ask for a box of condoms, bracing yourself for the humiliating question, "What size?"—and sometimes he trusted too much in luck. But Faith was one of the sweetest interludes in his ugly little life. Then she stopped calling, and Aubrey was frantic, wondering if someone else had come into her life or if her domineering mother had finally found them out. Then Faith was sent away. Just like that. She was disappeared, in that strange manner that young women were sometimes disappeared. There was talk. There was speculation. There was the usual round of merciless, vicious-tongued gossip all over Harman, as if people had nothing better to do. Which they didn't. Aubrey did the only thing he knew how to do—nothing. But it was a cowardly thing. He didn't call Faith's mother. He didn't ask where she had gone, though people murmured about an aunt in Edmonton, a good long piece away, which seemed appropriate under the circumstances.

And now this letter, which he could not even imagine replying to ("Hello, son! Long time no see!"). The boy seemed reasonably bright, probably well-educated. His letter was so respectful it was almost courtly. At least he didn't sound like one of those disreputable youths with the long hair and flapping pant legs that Aubrey kept seeing around town, the what-d'you-call-'ems, the hippies. Half of them weren't even in school, for God's sake, but spent all their time "hanging out," idling around, smoking their strange little hand-rolled cigarettes, playing guitars, and staging "be-ins" at the park.

This young man seemed to have the stamp of quality on him. But what did he want? Was he merely curious, or did he hate Aubrey for disappearing out of his life? Did he want money (good heavens, had he got a whiff of Min's fortune?), an apology, or to make up for lost time? And how was Aubrey supposed to pursue a "relationship," whatever that meant, with someone he didn't even know existed until a few minutes ago?

But worse things lurked, and this sickened Aubrey still more. There were the other times, the other women. The "lower companions," as they referred to them in AA circles. When Aubrey thought of what he had got himself into with Dot, it made him shiver with horror. Sober, he never would have given her the time of day. No, that was not quite true—but he never would have landed in her bed.

In those days Aubrey learned nothing from his mistakes. When conscience kicked up, he took a drink. And when Aubrey drank, it was like the old saying: "The man takes a drink. The drink takes a drink. The drink takes the man." Oblivion followed, which was exactly what he was seeking.

It is hard to follow one's conscience in a state of oblivion. Nearly impossible. So Aubrey made messes, terrible messes, dodged and fled, leaped out of the throes of advanced alcoholism just before it swallowed him alive, and settled into a life where nothing ever changes. And he prayed that all the dead bodies, the spectres of past damage, would remain safely buried.

And now, a hand burst up out of the soil of that graveyard, flailing around in mid-air to find something to grab on to, another hand to hold.

He turned the radio on, badly in need of escape. His mind began to unfocus, almost the way it had with the drink. As the tubes heated up he noticed an odour, hot fabric and dust, the smell of the past. Organ music swelled, and an announcer's florid voice intoned:

"*The Romance of Helen Trent.* In which we learn that although a woman is thirty-five, or even older, romance in life need not be over."

5.

Things were changing in Harman, and not for the better. Nobody noticed it more than Soapy Hudson, the usually amiable owner of Hudson's Lumberyard, a business he had inherited from his father Dan. It had started only about a year ago when some of these young people from the high school began to let their hair get scandalously long.

You couldn't even tell the boys from the girls any more, not from the back anyways, with the way their hair cascaded down to their shoulders or even right down their backs, like horses' tails. Soapy wouldn't have minded so much if they'd kept it clean. "No sir, I don't mind long hair, not as long as it's clean." But these young people, the ones he referred to as "hippie crap," seemed to pride themselves on not bathing. They sat around cross-legged in a big circle in Horace Gribble Memorial Park with their guitars, singing songs by some girly-looking character named Donovan: "First there is a mountain, then there is no mountain, then there is." "Wear your love like heaven." The girls made necklaces out of flowers and the boys passed the same cigarette around to everybody, as if they couldn't afford to buy their own. They even nailed a sign up over the gateway, rechristening the place as People's Park.

People, my ass. These kids didn't behave much more responsibly than animals. Didn't he find a couple of them copulating behind a stack of wet two-by-fours only last week? No romance. No preliminaries. No bottle of wine or dinner to ease the shock. Just get down there on the ground and do it.

In Soapy's day, if you wanted to do it badly enough, you got married, or if you couldn't stand the rigours of marriage, you secretly slipped five dollars to Helen Fox, the divorcee with the smart suits and the leopard skin pill-box hat. You didn't just lie down and do the dirty deed. It was almost as bad as self-abuse. If you did it (and nobody would admit they did), then you weren't proud of it, as these young people seemed to be. Young girls on "the pill." Some of them pregnant, their bellies sticking right out shamelessly, not even going away to visit Aunt Dora in Edmonton for a few months, the way it was supposed to happen when a girl got herself in trouble.

Soapy unlocked the front door of the office in a dark mind. He'd had to pick up butts off the ground where the couple had been going at it in their hideaway, and they weren't your regular cigarettebutts either, but twisty at the end. It took Soapy a minute to realize that these young people were smoking reefer like a bunch of gangsters, or worse, musicians. He found a few Baby Ruth wrappers trampled into the ground (marijuana being notorious for stimulating the appetite), but when he had to pry a disgusting object off the bottom of his shoe, it was the last straw. The thing was tied in a knot like an obscene grey balloon and so slimy that he didn't even want to touch it. He had to scrape it off his sole with a stick.

Soapy stood outside the office on Davison Street,

watching the slow, deliberate movements of the town of Harman on an ordinary day. Not that it seemed slow. The rest of the world may have moved in a blur by comparison, but Harmanites would have been deeply insulted if anyone referred to their community as "sleepy." Never mind that the vegetable man still insisted on driving a horse and wagon instead of a truck. He was Italian and couldn't help it. The *clop-clop-clopping* was soothing to listen to anyway. There was Mrs. Jamieson strolling down the street with her two mucous-nosed adenoidal brats, Denise and Randy, probably heading over to the Belgian bakery to catch up on all the latest dirt. And Mrs. Walker with her chic black poodle. Seventy years old and still meticulously dressed in what looked to be a very old but well-preserved Chanel suit. And for all her elegant appearance, teetering on her heels from her morning snort of sherry. Soapy wondered if she still pined for Shelton Gramercy, the great love of her life. But who hadn't the old dog slept with in this town at one time or another?

Thoughts of Shelton made him remember someone else, someone he wouldn't normally allow himself to think about. In fact it had been years since he had even let her cross his mind. But Gramercy had been her first love; everybody knew it, even though that harpy Min went and had her married off to the pansy hatter Robbie when she got herself in the family way.

He turned his head and, as if by some kind of evil magic, the object of his thoughts materialized right before his eyes. He blinked hard. It couldn't be her, but it was her, bearing down on him hard with her steamroller of a walk, as if she'd destroy everything in her path.

When Eileen clapped eyes on Soapy, you could

almost see an exclamation point forming above her head; she was that surprised. It was one of those moments when it was impossible to know how to react—a social vacuum, so to speak, a void where no usual rule of behaviour would suffice. So politeness rushed in to fill the gap.

"Eileen."

"Howard."

"What brings you to these parts? It's been years."

"I'm going to see Mother."

"Are you, now." Unspeakable thoughts rioted in Soapy's head. This was the woman with whom he had shared his bed—and more than that, his name—for two turbulent years. He could not censor the thought that rushed into his head, of that little breathless moaning sound she always made when they were going at it in bed. Before Eileen, Soapy hadn't realized that women had feelings like that. Not decent women, anyway. The memory flew into his head unbidden and flushed his face dark with embarrassment. Did Eileen remember their congress too, or had too many husbands blurred the memory into one big heaving tumble beneath the sheets?

"Blood is thicker than water." Cliches were good for filling the void, too.

"So you and Aubrey are speaking again."

"We'll see."

"He's a stubborn old cuss." He pulled out his pack of Salems and offered her one, which she took with finesse. Thank God for smoking and all its attendant rituals; it helped mitigate the agony of unwanted social encounters.

"No worse than you, Howard. How's the Mrs.?"

"She's fine." Soapy didn't mention that Alma had gained nearly a hundred pounds since they got married five years ago and now spent almost all her time hiding in the house, eating incessantly, as if working on her burgeoning flesh like a project. When Soapy saw her upper arms, he could not help but think of the yellowish shelf fungus that swelled overnight on trees.

But Eileen did look smart. Tall as she was, she knew how to dress, shoes matching her bag, jacket artfully cut to disguise her rather large hips. She had her hair in a radically different style from the high teased reddish puff of days gone by (what she called her "Carmel Quinn look," after the strident Irish entertainer whose voice could rattle glass). Now it was simply cut to chin length in the manner of Barbra Streisand, and looked stylish, if a little incongruous on a woman of a certain age. Soapy assumed that when Barbra Streisand hit fifty-odd she would show a little more dignity.

And she smelled good. The same old fragrance, Evening in Paris, which she would probably wear until the day she died.

"I hear she's put on a few pounds." Eileen looked directly into his eyes and blew out a lungful of smoke in a way that was downright intimidating.

"None of your concern, Leenie." How did she find these things out anyway? Was there a radar that went along with being female?

"She should try the Air Force Diet. Low carbohydrate. Sixty grams a day. Just don't eat bread and potatoes. You can lose five pounds in a week."

He looked her up and down. "Have you tried it lately?"

"Howard. Let's not get into a wrangle again."

"I'm not getting into a wrangle. It's just that you should practice what you preach."

"Yes, you should. And while you're at it, you should also fulfill your obligations."

"What are you saying, Eileen?"

"That if we're talking about practicing and preaching here, we shouldn't live in glass houses."

"What are you talking about?"

"Don't pretend you don't know. Are you in any position to criticize me about anything, Howard? It seems to me you stayed around just long enough to get me pregnant. Twice."

"Don't bring that up. The payments have always been right on time."

"Payments." Eileen snorted out a plume of smoke. Soapy thought that she looked like an angry horse. "As if the money will cover it. Two sons without a father . . ."

"Oh, they had a father all right. More than one."

"Well, what was I supposed to do? Raise them all on my own?"

"Eileen. Did it ever occur to you that you don't know how to hold a man?"

She didn't know what to say to this, or even exactly what it meant, except that somehow the mess of her marriages had been all her fault. She dragged on her cigarette to hide a pang of distress.

Then Soapy said something that took her by surprise.

"I'm sorry, Eileen. That was out of line."

"Well, Howard, there may be some truth in it."

"Not much. Maybe . . . your choices weren't always the best."

"Choices go both ways."

"I never regretted you, Leenie."

"You didn't?" A hint of tears thickened her voice.

"We had us some good times, didn't we?"

"We did. Between fights."

"And you've always been a good Mum to all those kids."

"Thank you, Howard." Then it was her turn to take him by surprise. She leaned over and planted a firm buss on his cheek that left a cherry kiss-mark. " I've got to go see Mother now. Take care of yourself, dear, and tell Alma about the diet."

"I will." He knew he wouldn't. He knew he'd go to Peck's Grocery and buy the usual bags of Korn Kurls and Cheez Twists his wife demanded daily. It kept the peace. But he would say anything to get away from Eileen now because she was having the same old effect on him that she always did. The last thing he wanted was for her to see the evidence, as she had an uncanny eye for these things, like an eagle spotting a trout in a stream half a mile away.

Eileen strode with great determination towards the old brick home of her childhood, bracing her spine for the coming encounter. Running into her ex-husband hadn't done much for her morale. And Mother could eat away at your confidence like termites in the foundation of an old house. Once more she would have to muster her power to endure.

There it was, the cat's-paw imprint she used to stick her finger in as a girl. Once she took wet clay and made a cast of it. She hesitated before swinging the door open to step into the dim front hall. The familiar air of home rushed out to surround her, a smell of old wicker, dust, and apple jelly sealed into jars with paraffin wax, a smell of cigar ashes and overripe muskmelon and Uncle Whit's coarse grey wool coat. Eileen's skin prickled with memory.

When she laid eyes on Aubrey he looked so much like the old pictures of Father that she wanted to take a step backwards. Same jutting ears that she used to call Red Sails in the Sunset. Same olive-tinged skin, green eyes, and coarse salt-and-pepper hair. Black Irish, only a little more swarthy and common.

Strangely, for a moment they looked at each other without saying anything. Aubrey saw a big middle-aged woman with rah-rah red lipstick and two curtains of hair on either side of her broad face, like the ears of a spaniel. And what was that smell? Scent, at her age, a cloud of it. Did the woman never give up hope?

"How is she?"

"Resting. She's had her breakfast."

"But she knows I'm coming."

"Of course." It was strange to launch into a conversation about Mother like this, with no preliminaries, not even a hello.

Eileen strode into the parlour, which looked eerily the same after years of absence. She stuck her tongue out at Buck, blew at him to clear the dust, then shook her head when she saw the old radio still there beside the rocker. "Buy a new one, Aub. Don't be so cheap." She flipped it on and twiddled the dial. "Get on up," a gronky black baritone voice intoned, "and sock it to me." Eileen began snapping her fingers to the obscene honkings of a saxophone.

"Eileen, for heaven's sake. At your age."

"At least I'm not making myself old like you are."

"Leenie. That's not fair."

"Even Mother's younger than you. At least she's still got some life in her."

"And how would you know?"

Aubrey had her there. For a second she didn't know what to say. Then she swept past him. "I'll go and find out," she said.

Aubrey heard her tap on Mother's door. Then she went in, closing it behind her. He tried not to listen in, but the temptation was just too much for him. He could hear their individual voices, the rise and fall of them. He could hear what sounded like awkward pauses. Then a subtle rise in the volume of the conversation, as if they were arguing about something. He could clearly make out, "But you were never *there!*" and was shocked to realize that Eileen had said it, not Min.

Then the voices died down again. They sounded almost placating. Murmurs of—what, affection? Aubrey strained to imagine what they were actually saying, hating himself for needing to know. Then, after only about five minutes in Min's room, Eileen burst out again (and maybe it was only her size and stature that made her appear to "burst"—she could hardly help that). She looked slightly red-eyed but composed.

"I suppose you want a full report. Or did you hear everything already?"

"It didn't go well?" Eileen was surprised at how gentle his tone was. It threw her off. How hard it was to stay angry with him. Almost impossible.

"What did you expect, with Mother? You should know that better than anyone. Her main pleasure in life is criticizing. And judging. And telling me what a mess I've made of my life. As if her own is such a model. She gets her jollies from that dirty old man, that Dr. Bliss, feeling around and doing his examinations." Aubrey wondered how she knew. But Eileen was no fool, and could pick up a lot just from Min's tone of voice.

"Mother likes to ruffle people's feathers, Leenie. But she's got a good heart. She's getting near the end of her life, trying to put her affairs in order."

"Aha." Eileen pulled out another cigarette. "Her will. I suppose that's why people think I'm here. Well, I don't give a rip about the money. I just don't want her to be able to say I abandoned her."

"That's good of you, Eileen." Aubrey was trying, and it touched her. For a second neither of them knew what to say.

"I should let you get back to work," she said, her voice a little shaky.

"It's just the usual thing, anyway. Taking inventory. The same old pile of boards."

"Aub, why don't you—"

He held up his hand and she stopped.

"Do you still see Pearl?"

"We go to the opera."

"Do you still go to meetings?"

"I don't need the meetings, Eileen." She meant AA, where he'd met Pearl years ago.

"But it might give you a bit of a social life. Better than keeping company with a godawful old woman and a dead dog."

This should have irritated Aubrey, even infuriated him, but his dour face stretched into a wicked grin, like Mother's. There's hope for him yet, Eileen thought.

"Have you talked to Barlow and Dwight?"

"For God's sake, woman, what is this, an inquisition?" The grin vanished. Obviously the topic of his twin brothers was still sensitive territory.

"Well, you'll be happy to know they're as oddball as ever. Must run in the family. Get a housekeeper, Aubrey! I see dust all over the place."

"I love you too, Eileen." Though his voice dripped with sarcasm, she knew that he meant it. She grimaced at him, blew him an air-kiss, grabbed her smart bag, and strode out the door, leaving Aubrey standing in a thick cloud of Evening in Paris.

6.

One of the open secrets of Harman was that Guillaume's Belgian bakery, social nucleus of the entire community, wasn't really Belgian at all. Shemp Gribble, younger brother of the town's most famous son, had blown the whistle on Guy some years ago by spilling the news that his grandparents had originally come from Luxembourg, not Belgium.

"Why not come right out with it and call him Dutch?" Mrs. Wilhelmina Peck, stout iron-haired matron of Peck's Grocery, had snorted.

"Don't be silly, Willie. Belgium is nowhere near Holland." Geography had never been one of Shemp's stronger subjects.

"We are speaking of the Netherlands. Belgium is just south of the region," Willie pointed out, tracing an invisible map in the air with a sausage-like finger tipped with a vicious red nail.

"Anyways, he ain't even *from* Belgium. His people are from Luxembourg, this little two-bit country away off by itself."

"Luxembourg borders on the southeastern tip of Belgium. There is a certain affinity between the citizens of Luxembourg, Belgium, and the Netherlands, a sort of regional similarity. Dutch is Dutch, I always say."

"But he don't even grow tulips!" Shemp guffawed. Mrs. Peck was mildly irritated. That Shemp could be so coarse. And his grammar—atrocious! It was a mystery to them all in the good town of Harman how the same family could have produced Shemp (born Samuel, but later rechristened because of his strong resemblance to the least popular member of the Three Stooges) and that lovely Percival, who went on to distinguish himself by writing seventeen books.

"He don't even wear wooden shoes!" There was no stopping Shemp once he got cranked up. Mrs. Peck tried her best to ignore him. But when Ethel McConnaughey the incorrigible gossip came in to the store later that day, Wilhelmina Peck just happened to let slip the information that the Belgian Bakery wasn't really Belgian at all.

"*Dutch!* You don't mean it."

"Why don't they just come right out and say it?"

"Oh, you know why, Willie."

The two women exchanged a look that said it all, immediately damning anyone with the vaguest connection to Holland for at least a three-hundred-mile radius.

There was a sort of catechism that everyone followed in Harman. It helped them make sense of a complex and rapidly changing world. The shocking rigidity of this set of unspoken rules completely escaped them, or most of them. If you were Dutch, you were pushy. You were loud. You were arrogant, garrulous. You had to have your own way. Why, look at that Wim Van der Hoot down Factory Road, living in the worst part of town, broken baby buggies and a sandbox full of cat droppings right in his backyard, yet acting like some sort of prince among men, and couldn't that wife of his with the seven little kids like stairsteps do with a good bath now and again?

"And they're supposed to be clean," Willie would sniff.

That was the Dutch, all tied up and settled, and there was no arguing with it. Jews weren't even talked about. There were no Jews in Harman anyway, but quite a number of people besides Percy Gribble had changed their names, and didn't that give them away right there? Once a Negro moved in beside the Jamiesons on Eagle Street, but he'd had the sense to quickly move out again. Every time he left the house he felt his skin turning to frost. It was those stares. They were palpable, lowering the temperature to a point below freezing.

And if you were a homosexual—may God have mercy on your soul.

Not much of this bothered the good people of Harman, except for a few conscientious souls like Guy the secret Dutchman. And then there were those who simply rose above it all, like Shelton Gramercy.

People wondered why he stayed on in Harman when he could have lived anywhere in the world—Paris, Rome, even Luxembourg, if that really was a country. Seventeen best-selling novels over a period of thirty-odd years had given him his ticket to freedom. But still he stayed on in the old Gribble place that Horace had built with his own hands, spending hours a day at his typewriter, trying to capture the elusive enigma of the human condition in his stories of lust and intrigue set in a small community in southwestern Ontario. In the imaginations of countless thousands of readers, Elmsdale had become more significant than an actual place. It was better than a place—it was a landscape of the mind, an Anytown, an Everytown that snared the hearts of readers, because it made them realize that the miserably narrow values of their own communities were downright liberal compared to the clanged-shut, bear-trap, sealed-tomb small minds of the folks of Elmsdale.

And the sex, the sex! It was as if the men of Elmsdale all had a third testicle, or the women effused an exotic and irresistible musk through their very skin. Anglican ministers still wearing their Sunday vestments rutted away feverishly with married schoolteachers. Men in their fifties with grey chest hair and swollen prostates seduced shy, virginal maidens of sixteen. Somehow Gramercy made everyone's most furtive and delicious fantasies come true. Even better, the horrible repercussions these characters suffered made their rampant sins acceptable, even desirable, to show what happens when you start following these lower impulses, which all decent people know you're supposed to suppress, thank you very much. If, in fact, you have them at all.

It was quite an event in Harman when Shelton Gramercy was out and about, going for a stroll with his elegant borzoi or dropping by the bakery for a cup of coffee. Like so many artists, the man needed his privacy and usually kept to himself (except for the women). Though everybody knew where he lived, it was an unspoken rule that no one would tip off a stranger as to his whereabouts. Once his fans figured out that there was no such place as Elmsdale (a great disappointment, as it would have been such a thrill to have our very own Gomorrah right here in Ontario), they began to do some digging and eventually came up with Harman. The standard response to the question, "Can you tell me where I can find Shelton Gramercy?" was "Never heard of the man" (or the slightly more honest "There's no one here by that name"). Well, wasn't it true? Had he ever legally changed his name from Gribble? It wasn't even a lie, just a protective strategy. Every once in a while someone slipped through the safety net and ambushed the poor man as he walked out of the Harman Public Library or Sid's Bar and Grill. There was the time a brash young reporter jumped out from behind the bushes and snapped his photo before Gramercy could stop him. "Sit," he commanded his borzoi, Ranulf. Then he struck a dignified pose. No use looking shabby in the papers. Not that he cared a whit about appearances.

Now deep into his seventies, at an age when most men would be sitting around the cracker barrel swapping pointless stories, Gramercy was still hard at it, in more ways than one. Over the years there had been quite a number of women, but it always seemed that when they reached a certain age—usually around thirty-five—they mysteriously vanished, tearfully packing up to go back to Mother in Listowel. Soon another model would appear, younger and blonder than the one before. He even had several children by these liaisons, but they had a way of disappearing too. He'd been married once, way back in the stone age, and then, of course, there was that business with Eileen Connar . . . but look what happened there. You could hardly blame a man when his woman turned out to be bad seed.

Shelton Gramercy clanged open the door of Guy's Belgian Bakery and inhaled the heavy, almost erotic scent of newly baked loaves. He commanded the dog to sit and strode over to the counter to order a coffee and a meringue.

The old man had changed somewhat from the dapper days of his youth and now dressed casually in tweedy leather-patched cardigans, corduroy pants, and open-necked shirts. But still he commanded respect in a way that was downright eerie.

"Mr. Gramercy." Guy greeted him with all the delight of meeting a celebrity.

"Guy."

"How's the book coming?"

"It's coming." Gramercy could be laconic to a fault.

"How's the missus?"

"She's not my missus. Or my mistress either."

"I meant no disrespect, Mr. Gramer—"

"Then just leave me alone."

Guy was not offended. One must allow for the quirks of genius. The great man took his chartreuse-tinted meringue and viscous black coffee over to a table in the far corner. The borzoi obediently followed, flopping down beside his master, who pulled out a spiral notebook, peered at it intensely, and began to scribble.

This was why Guy could never stay angry at the man. It was fascinating, watching him write. What was in those notebooks? Chapters of his latest novel? A personal diary? Observations on the small-town life which seethed all around him, feeding lifelike details into the mythic world of Elmsdale? Dot claimed she'd glimpsed a page over his shoulder once when he lit her cigarette. "Two quarts of milk. Ipana toothpaste. Vel soap. Suppositories. A grocery list. The man's just like the rest of us." Others insisted it was blatant pornography that he sent over to Europe to be published under another name. Once when he went to the bathroom to unload some of Guy's poisonous coffee, Mrs.

McConnaughey tried to sneak a look, but the borzoi sprang up and bit her in the calf. The threat of a lawsuit led to a generous settlement out of Gramercy's own pocket.

He settled in for a long session of writing with his usual furrowed scowl. Gramercy had a way of giving off a sense of importance like a vapour, palpable, almost visible. It impressed publishers. It sold copies at book signings. It had a mystical effect on the knee joints of young women, who were rendered gooey at a glance. It was all part of the thick moss of legend that had gradually accumulated around the man.

The bell clanged again, and he winced in irritation. Damn these interruptions. This was even worse than at home, where Agnes kept nattering on about the mortgage, the bills. He'd peel off a few hundred-dollar bills from his wad and hand them to her, but still she wanted to talk, an irritating habit.

The form of a lanky young man dressed in a woven cotton shirt and faded jeans appeared in the doorway, haloed in sunlight. On his back was a small brown canvas rucksack. He stood there for a moment exuding uncertainty and strangeness—new to Harman, obviously. But when Gramercy eyed him up and down more closely, he felt a thrill of shock and a sudden acceleration of the heart.

Jesus, he thought.

Anyone would react the same way. (That is, anyone with a decent upbringing, not including those Godless Hindus who ran the hardware store.) The resemblance was uncanny and had a visceral effect. The long, fine wavy brown hair almost seemed to give off light, and the soft full beard and tender blue eyes caused an immediate ache of recognition, of nostalgia. This young man, whoever he was, could have served as the model for the portrait of Jesus that hung on the wall of every Sunday school room in every church in every town in this great wide country. Hymns from eons ago, deeply recorded in the vaults of his memory, began to blare in Gramercy's mind: "Red and yellow, black and white, they are precious in his sight, Jesus loves the little children of the world." "A sunbeam, a sunbeam, Jesus wants me for a sunbeam." "When he cometh, when he cometh, to make up his jewels . . ."

"Good day," the young man said to Gramercy, sounding surprisingly articulate and self-possessed. He pulled up a chair and sat, and the borzoi came and rested his head in his lap, sighing deeply. "May I ask you where I can find the nearest hotel?"

"When mothers of Salem their children brought to Jesus . . ." Gramercy tried to shake off the phantom hymn. "There's Sam's place over on Elm. But it's not up to much. And Sid rents out rooms above the bar, but I don't think you'd want to go there. If the rats don't get you, the cockroaches will. New in town?"

"Yes, I guess you could say that."

"Staying long?"

"You might say I'm on a mission."

Gramercy's pupils dilated. "Listen, young man, I've an extra room in my house. Why don't you come and stay with me?" Never mind what Agnes would say when he brought Jesus home with him. This appealed to his writerly sense of adventure. The young stranger would make a dandy character in *Jest of Heaven*, his eighteenth novel, which right now was running a little slow.

"I'm embarrassed by your generosity. You don't even know me."

"Aha, my good man, there's where you're wrong. I feel as if I've known you all my life."

Clang, and the door burst open again. There she was, Dot, the last person anyone would want to see at a time like this.

She dropped all her bags on the floor with a thud.

"Christ!" she exclaimed.

"Pleased to meet you, ma'am." The young man extended his hand.

"And you'd be?"

"Bob."

"I'm Dot." She looked completely flustered. "You look like . . ."

". . . you could use a coffee." Guy practically ran over to Bob with a mug and a glistening pink spudnut. "They're on the house."

Bob smiled beatifically at them both. He had beautiful teeth, well-kept, very even and white. The dog's tail swung slowly back and forth. Any new person in Harman was an event, but the Second Coming was like hitting the jackpot.

"You've all been so kind. And I don't even know your name," he said to Shelton in amazement.

An instant of hesitation.

"Percy Gribble." Gramercy shook his hand.

Guy and Dot exchanged a look. Jesus and the novelist put their heads together and became locked in a long, murmuring private conversation while people came and went. Soapy Hudson, in for the usual two dozen doughnuts that he'd never get a taste of, muttered a comment about "hippie crap" until Guy silenced him with a sharp look. Ethel McConnaughey nearly had a heart attack on the spot.

"It's not," she whispered.

"We don't think so," Guy said.

"But he's the very image . . ."

"I only serve the best," Guy said smugly.

"You don't suppose he has, you know. What I mean is . . ."

"Powers?"

"I'm not sure I'd put it that way."

"I'll give him a glass of water. See if he can turn it into Chablis."

"Guy, you're terrible." She giggled. "Still, he does have a certain . . . you know . . ."

"You're right, Ethel. But better not tell anyone. Remember what Reverend Sanderson said last Sunday in the gospel lesson, when that little girl was raised from the dead?"

"'Tell no one what has happened,'" she murmured, her brain buzzing. Guy suppressed a smile at the thought of Ethel keeping anything to herself.

The two men left together, the dog trotting at Bob's heels in a state of rapture. The sight of Shelton Gramercy strolling down the avenue with the Son of Man was a little too much for the residents of Harman to absorb. "He does have interesting friends," they said to one another. "Remember that—what was his name anyway? That Morley Callaghan fellow, stayed one whole summer. And the actor, that chap from Stratford? Saw him on TV once. Played a Klingon on Star Trek." From famous actors, it was but a small step to the man from Galilee. And it revitalized the town, gave them all something new to talk about. The talk washed over Aubrey Connar, as most of this idle gossip did. He was sure the presence of this strange young man had nothing at all to do with him.

7.

Cloppa, cloppa. Cloppa, cloppita, cloppa. It was a sound that soon would be all but extinct in the world. But, of course, no one knew that at the time. It was just the sound of early morning in a small town, the large shaggy hooves of an old grey horse lazily hitting the pavement. The horse knew the way, so Cookie, the driver, didn't have to do very much of anything. Just sat up there in the wagon with Old Sal on a loose rein. She'd stop automatically in front of every house, and Cookie would climb down and deposit the day's order—a glass quart bottle of homo milk, a pint of half-and-half, a pound of Lakewood's butter in wax paper— in a small cupboard at the back. It had always been that way, for as long as anyone could remember. In most cases they didn't even have to leave a note. Cookie already knew what they needed.

The phone rang in the Connar household. It was early, far too early for normal folk to be up and about on a week end, unless of course you'd been up all night doing God knows what. Aubrey, constitutionally incapable of just let-ting it ring, dragged his stiff body out of bed and stalked to the phone, cursing and mumbling all the way.

"Hello."

"*Gunther,*" a drunken voice boomed.

"Go to bed, old woman!"

"Is Gunther there?" A hundred thousand incinerated cigarettes lurked behind the croaking rasp of her voice.

"There's . . . no . . . one . . . here . . . by . . . that . . . name."

"You don't need to be so short with me, young man. I know I dialed correctly." Aubrey was surprised to hear her speak in complete sentences. At least this time there was no singing.

"Then the telephone must be broken."

"*A-hyuh-ahyuh-hyuh-hyuh-hyuh-hlblblblt.*" The hollow, booming cannon-fire of her coughing literally vibrated with loose phlegm. Aubrey thought he heard a parrot squawk in the background. The woman was insane. He hung up before she could take a deep breath and start a new round. A moment later, the phone rang again. He lifted the receiver, then banged it down as hard as he could.

Speaking of parrots, it would soon be time to feed Min. The old bird was hatching something out in that cunning old mind of hers. A plan as evil and insidious as a plague of fleas. Seeing Eileen again had done something to her. Made her go all nostalgic for what never was—family harmony. Aubrey knew Barlow and Dwight would have something to do with it, and God only knew who else.

Aubrey made a policy of not thinking about Barlow and Dwight, which of course meant that he thought of them many times a day. It was like that with blood kin, something in the genetic code that made thoughts come up unbidden. To Aubrey's relief, they had lived in Horgansville for many years now, and who ever wanted to go to Horgansville anyway? They didn't even have a movie theatre, or a Kentucky Fried Chicken, or a municipal swimming pool (never mind that Harman's was all of four feet deep and only operated in August). The conditions were downright primitive. Seven hundred and twelve people—pathetic! Harman's two thousand and fifty-eight made it a seething metropolis by comparison.

Barlow and Dwight had gained a lot of mileage out of their identical status in their childhood and youth. Ancient Harman schoolteachers, toothless and prune-lipped, still reminisced about Barlow working off Dwight's detention for blowing up the principal's desk with a four-incher, or Dwight showing up for Barlow's date with Gwendolyn Gosford, the prettiest girl in Normal School. *Such a couple of wags. None too bright, but we'll forgive them that. Aubrey got all the brains, didn't he, for all the good it did him. Slinging lumber for Soapy while the twins are selling insurance, a real gentleman's job. And I hear they have a real nice duplex in Horgansville. Married to sisters, aren't they?* That's how the talk went, until it degenerated into terrible stories about Aubrey's drinking that dated back twenty-five years.

But there were even worse murmurings about the twins, such as the absurd and patently untrue rumour that they had been born conjoined—"Siamese twins, right out of *Ripley's Believe It or Not*"—attached in a highly unlikely place. Never mind that this phenomenon had never been heard of in all of medical history. The rumour had apparently started when, at three months, the boys developed a condition called phimosis from unusually tight foreskins and had to be circumcized, leaving them sore and squalling for weeks. This somehow got convoluted into a story far more lurid in content. Why hadn't Min taken those twins out of the house for so long? And when she finally did, why did they lie so close together in that buggy? "Joined at the willie," the gossipmongers concluded. And at three months, the legend continued, Min, fed up with raising a sideshow act, had snipped them apart with a pair of garden shears.

Idle gossip, of course, but it followed the twins around. People continued to joke about it, particularly when the two boys entered their teens and began to court young women. Gwennie Gosford never understood why someone left a magnifying glass in her book satchel at Normal School before her date with Barlow. And when they finally married those unfortunate-looking Braddock sisters, stolid and plain as turnips, everyone concluded that with their looks, the girls probably weren't too fussy about what they got.

When no children issued from the double union, it seemed to verify the wicked story. Can't sire sons with half a member, no sir, people snickered, ignoring the fact that Barlow and Dwight had suffered a vicious form of mumps after puberty and were rendered sterile. Didn't Eileen's excessive fertility make up for the fact? Weren't her eleven children enough of a sop to all the wagging tongues of Harman?

Aubrey shuffled towards Min's room, the Pep flakes swimming in milk on the tray, a fly walking across the skin of the blackened banana. He wondered if she'd died again in the night, or what. No such luck: "Aubrey!" she cried from behind the door in the kind of annoyingly shrill, querulous voice which is unique to the very old. He sighed and let himself in. As he was setting down the tray on her bedside table, a bluish, clawlike hand shot out, grabbed his collar, and pulled his face up close to hers.

"Aubrey. We need to talk."

He could smell her breath, as musty as if she'd been

chewing flies, and her veiny red eyeballs practically made contact with his.

"About what, Mother? Not the will again. I thought changing it once a week was enough."

"About the reunion."

"The re-what?"

"Aubrey. Seeing Eileen again made me realize something." Oh my Lord, she was about to cry. It was terrible when Min cried. Snot poured out of her sharp nose. She wheezed. She couldn't get her breath. She wanted brandy and a hot water bottle for her stomach.

"Don't cry, Mother."

"Don't cry, Mother. That's easy for you to say. Eileen is flesh of my flesh, bone of my bone . . ."

"Well, she's my blood kin too, but it doesn't make her any easier to get along with."

"Aubrey. This family is a disgrace. Everyone in Harman talks about it, the way you don't talk to your brothers any more, as if they've done something terrible. The way you cut poor Eileen out of your life all those years ago."

"Cut her out of my—"

"Don't you deny it. She's had to raise all those children practically by herself."

"You make it sound as if all this is my fault. There's a phone right beside your bed, Mother. Nothing's stopping you from calling Barlow and Dwight yourself."

"I already did."

Aubrey's stomach fell through the floor.

"They're coming to the reunion. They promised. All fourteen of Eileen's children will be there, too. I'm not long for this world, Aubrey."

"Oh, Mother. You've been saying that for ten years."

"I'll be ninety. Then I'll be worm food. Without the rest of the family by my side, you'd probably take it upon yourself to bury me in the backyard. Or have me stuffed, like Buck."

Aubrey turned away to stifle a guffaw. He could picture it.

"Do you even know what my wishes are? Did you realize that I want to be cremated? No memorial service. No, not for me, though that bugger Nin Sanderson's been waiting for me to kick off for years now so he can spin all his favourite stories at the pulpit. A pack of lies. No, Aubrey, I don't want a service. Just a reunion, all of us together in one place. At Gribble Park. We'll get the Harman Kiltie Band to play in the bandshell. Never mind that they're Scotch; we'll make them play some decent Irish things. We'll have a dance. Games for the kiddies."

"A pie-eating contest? Alma Hudson would win hands down."

He could see her mouth curl in an effort not to smile.

"Aubrey, I haven't much time."

"So this way," he said, "you can make up your mind who gets the money by how everyone behaves at the reunion."

"This has nothing to do with money."

"Sentiment, then? I can't believe this, Min. When did you get so soft?"

"Don't call me Min." But now she really was crying, and it wasn't that awful stage-Irish crying either. Her face was becoming congested with real anguish. "I'll soon be dead," she murmured, "and I hardly know my own children."

"Mother."

"You're the worst of all. In a shell all the time. You never tell me your real thoughts."

"I didn't think you wanted me to." But it made him acutely uncomfortable. And guilty. Had he really been that closed? Is this what duty does to people—dries them up at the source, so that they no longer know how to live from the heart?

"There's still time," Min said softly, and then Aubrey knew it was pointless to resist. He'd have to stop not thinking about Barlow and Dwight (which took a lot of energy) and start thinking about them again (which would take even more). He'd have to actually meet Eileen's brood, the whole thundering herd. How many ex-husbands would be invited? And would they bring their current spouses, too? Did this mean Robbie Davison would show up with his "business partner" Sean Stanigan, also known as Sean the Sissy? Aubrey's head reeled at the possibilities.

"I've told Eileen," Min said, looking calmer now.

"That means the whole county knows."

"She's making some calls." *Making some calls?* Aubrey could only imagine. Eileen knew where all the bodies were buried in her brother's past. Knew the names of all the women, even the ones Aubrey had long ago forgotten. The letter from that young man, that Robert Douglas Hemphill, still haunted him. Might not be a grain of truth in his story; Aubrey hadn't answered it, and had no intention of doing so.

"All right, Mother, you win."

"I don't ask for much, do I?"

Aubrey rolled his eyes.

"Get me out of bed, will you. I need to use the toilet." This was followed by the usual tugs, grunts, and heaves.

Finally she was upright. Aubrey gave her a gentle shove in the right direction, and she began to walk in the tiny Chinese foot-bound steps of the very elderly. She disappeared into the bathroom—thank God, she could still manage that without his help—and shut the door behind her.

Aubrey hadn't thought about taking a drink for a very long time. But now he thought about it. In fact he did more than think: he could almost feel the first shot burning down his throat like molten gold. He knew he wouldn't do it— not after all these years, not after the warning from Dr. Bliss that his liver looked like a six-month pregnancy: "Next stop, cirrhosis." But the thought came into his head, and there it was. He and Pearl hadn't been to an AA meeting in years; wasn't it the same message they heard in church? Trust God, clean up the messes you make, help others. Common sense. Never mind that alcoholics never seemed to have any. "Angels with one wing," they used to call each other at meetings, only able to fly if they hung on to each other.

Maybe he'd go to a meeting one of these days and surprise everyone. Not that there'd be anyone left in the group who'd remember him. And the ones who had relapsed were all dead. Aubrey had heard from Shemp Gribble that the Golden Slippers group had been infiltrated by a bunch of young people. These men weren't even out of their thirties. What were they doing getting sober? But it got worse. There were women in the group now, four of them, upsetting the balance completely. It was getting so's the guys couldn't even swear.

But Aubrey decided that he'd think about it. There were rough times ahead, and God knew how many nasty surprises. Unless he stayed sober, he knew he didn't stand a chance.

8.

It wasn't true, what they said about Horgansville. You could get chicken there. Perfectly good chicken. All right, it came in a cardboard box, not a bucket. And it wasn't fried, but "broasted," which meant that the skin didn't ooze grease when you bit into it. Fry King on States Avenue did a good business in broasted chicken with french fries, made up fresh every day from the real potato, none of this frozen nonsense. And they didn't need a Colonel because they had Salem Alderman.

Salem didn't just own the Fry King; he embodied it, his considerable bulk wrapped in a pristine white apron as he moved with the whale-like grace of the very overweight from kitchen to dining room to takeout counter, making sure the chicken was cooked to his satisfaction and his customers were happy. He wasn't alone. His pepper-haired stump of a wife, Stella, moved even more briskly, giving off a sense of holy purpose, as if chicken were her mission.

People didn't come to the Fry King for the food, which was mediocre at best. They came for Salem and Stella, for a taste of the kind of caring parenthood they might not have experienced in childhood. Ah, the ache in such people. The incompleteness. They had no idea these yawning needs were being met when they went for chicken and french fries and Stella's garish cherry pie that could have been bound with glue. But when Friday night rolled around they'd say to each other, "Let's go to Fry King," and somehow it always seemed like a very good idea.

Horgansville wasn't like Harman at all, oh no sir it wasn't. Every community has its own private cosmos, its universe. For one thing, Horgansville still had some elm trees left. "As if we needed more proof about the Dutch," a sour-tongued matron would say, "just look at what they've done to our trees." And in other ways, too, it was way ahead of Harman. The milk was delivered by truck. Had been since 1965. Heartbroken old men climbed down from their wagons for the last time, knowing that they would never work again. And a shiny new fleet of trucks was brought in, with young men driving them. Progress.

Horgansville had a Dramatic Society. Harman didn't. In fact Harman had so little culture that some of its citizens had to drive all the way to Toronto just to go to the opera. But Horgansville made its own culture, putting on lively productions of *Our Town* and *Arsenic and Old Lace* in the high school gymnasium. The place would be packed. Where else could you see the mayor, the head librarian, and the school janitor treading the boards, making complete fools of themselves while everybody cheered?

Horgansville even had refugees. (Escapees, some people liked to call them.) Most of them were Connars. Everyone knew how those nice twin brothers had been driven out of Harman by that awful sot of a brother, that Aubrey who wasn't even married. The twins were married—never mind that their wives weren't much to look at; at least they were clean and decent and kept a spotless house. No children there, something went wrong somewhere along the line; there was an accident or an operation or something, and it affected the twins' ability to, well, you know. Let's not go into the details. But they all seemed to get along well in their tidy little duplex on Alcorn Street. The men had good jobs and the women knew how to keep quiet.

It was a bit of a shock for people to see Barlow and Dwight for the first time, especially in the last few years when Barlow, five minutes older than his brother, had aged so much and grown so stout. Meanwhile Dwight the young upstart had gone on that Air Force diet that everyone was talking about, started doing those 5BX calisthenics, and lost something in the neighbourhood of seventy-five pounds. The result was identical twins who looked almost nothing alike.

But that wasn't the only change in Dwight. "Looks like a goddamn hippie," Salem once muttered to Stella, and Stella's only comment was, "I don't mind long hair so long as it's clean." Dwight had become infected with the strange fever that had already swept through the youth of the town. Undignified, for a man his age. It started with the wide ties, then the bright colours, then flared pants that made him look ridiculous, and then—the final straw—letting his hair go past his shirt collar until it virtually curled.

It was different in 1967, the Centennial year, when men let all sorts of hair sprout and curl in strange places: Centennial sideburns, Centennial moustaches, even the odd full beard, which Stella claimed was inspired more by laziness than patriotic fervour. Stu Danville even grew a Centennial eyebrow, no longer bothering to shave them apart. But all that nonsense died down when the celebration was over. Then, a whole year later, Dwight took it upon himself to grow a moustache to match the long hair. Not a properly trimmed moustache like Don Ameche's, but one of those droopy things that made him look like a Mexican bandit. Some folks in the town admitted that they sort of liked it. They said it looked "mod." Others held their comments, believing Dwight had gone off the rails and next might start smoking reefer and chasing around after younger women.

Sadie didn't seem to mind, but then did Sadie mind anything? Her sister, Sara Ray, was the more outspoken of the two, which meant that if you stomped on her foot as hard as you could, she might say, "Ouch." Sadie seemed to be so grateful for being rescued from spinsterhood that she would never ask for anything again. The story around Horgansville was that the two drew straws to decide which brother to marry, and Sadie got the short straw. Everybody knew Barlow was the responsible one, serious in demeanour, impressive in girth. Barely cracked a smile, when that Dwight had a wicked sense of humour and played practical jokes on his colleagues at Barnstable Insurance—glued pens to their desks, left whoopee cushions on their chairs during important meetings. There was even a rumour going around that he had a tattoo somewhere on his body. "Must be a lot smaller now," said Stella.

One evening Dwight looked over at Sadie—it was a Friday night—and said, "Let's go to Fry King." Never mind that he said this virtually every Friday night; there was a certain ritual, a procedure to be followed.

"I was going to make fish," Sadie said in a weary voice.

"We can have it tomorrow."

"Friday's fish day."

"Can't we make an exception?"

Sadie would sigh. Not object. Not make a sour face. Just sigh. Dwight had had his way again, but at a cost. So in a sense, Sadie had won. She knew this. She kept track. It was her power.

Sadie used to be Catholic, a lot more Catholic than her sister Sara Ray, who went through the motions but never took to it particularly. Sadie was still Catholic in a faded, say-nothing way, and kept her rosary in a jewel case, and crossed herself whenever she prayed. "He's marrying a goddamned papist," Min had thundered, refusing to go to the wedding.

Just to be extra infuriating, she *did* go to Barlow's wedding a few months later. Sara Ray Braddock was different, Min reasoned. She didn't wear her Catholicism on her sleeve. Neither did Sadie, but Min never made much sense even at the best of times. She only got in one dig during the whole wedding. At the reception, when the chicken was served, Min said in a loud voice, "Give me the Pope's nose."

"I'll have to change my clothes," Sadie said with that little drag in her voice. Translation: Look what a bother you're putting me through.

"Nonsense. You're fine the way you are."

"This is a housedress, not a town dress." The housedress was pale blue, with little pictures of clocks all over it.

"Suit yourself." Dwight had on a red and blue madras plaid shirt, red suspenders, and royal blue flared pants in polyester doubleknit.

So Sadie changed into a pale grey dress with little

pictures of poodles all over it. Not quite a Sunday-best dress (and like so many faded Catholics, Sadie went to the United Church, probably to keep Min happy), but nevertheless one of her nicest. She had ordered it out of the back of *TV Guide* magazine for $17.99, and it had come all the way from Quebec. Sadie loved to send away for things; it was one of her few indulgences.

She even put on a dab of makeup—a line of brow pencil over each eye (though she didn't pluck them bald—that was too "out" even for Sadie) and a dot of cherry lipstick, which she smeared by rubbing her lips together. It made her feel a trifle wicked.

Friday night in Horgansville. Late spring. Almost, but not quite, lapsing into summer. A slow, warm slide like the lapsing of a woman's virtue. Dogs on the sidewalk, lying on their sides, panting. Some children already running around in shorts, knees grey with dirt. A red 1956 Thunderbird streaking past with the windows open, radio blaring, "Hot town, summer in the city, back of my neck gettin' dirt 'n' gritty." Dwight reached for Sadie's hand as they strolled over to Fry King on States Avenue (Barlow was using the car tonight, an ancient Studebaker which the twins frugally shared, to go to his Kiwanis Club meeting). It gave Sadie the hint of a shock. She wondered what might come next and her heartbeat increased a little, shocking her even more. Public displays of affection were unseemly in an old married couple, but also, Sadie had to admit, kind of romantic. Her body flinched slightly in half-pleasant, half-aversive anticipation of the sex that would probably come later on in the evening. Then she realized what was happening to her and clamped her pelvic muscles tight.

Dwight felt natty and young. More than just his appearance had changed in recent months. Ever since losing all that weight he'd been getting some yeasty ideas in his head, like the thought of travelling. He asked Sadie if she'd like to go with him to Ailsa Craig to visit an old school chum and she said, "What about our budget? Haven't you spent enough already on new clothes?" Sadie was always trying to put a cork in Dwight's newfound effervescence. Then he had the idea they'd go Up North. Lake of Bays, maybe. The wilds of Muskoka. Sadie thought he was starting to go crazy. She could picture him going around with no shirt on, exuding male sweat. The thought of it made her shudder.

Things like going to Fry King on a Friday night, little concessions like that, might placate the madness, keeping major change from threatening Sadie's small, astringently snug world. Secretly, in a place she wouldn't even admit to, she was glad she didn't have to cook.

On pulling open the door of the restaurant, a certain familiar air rushed out to envelop them, a heavy air saturated with hot grease and cigarette smoke. It made them both salivate in anticipation. Going to a restaurant for a meal when you already had perfectly good food at home was almost shamefully decadent. Knowing Dwight, now that he was done with his diet, he might even order a piece of Stella's glutinous cherry pie. Sadie always felt it was more prudent after a restaurant meal to have dessert at home. It kept the cost down.

"Folks!" Stella exclaimed, bustling about in her immaculate white apron. She looked like a psychiatric nurse Dwight had seen years and years ago, when he was visiting Uncle Whit in the hospital during his final, raving days. She gave off the same palpable aura of care for the less fortunate. "Come and sit down. Where'd you get that dress, Sadie? It's cute. You look smart tonight. And you, Dwight, well, gosh sakes, don't you look mod?" She fingered one of his suspenders, then gave it a snap. Sadie was mildly annoyed.

"The wife's tired of cooking." It was just true enough to increase her annoyance. "Besides, it's Friday night. Time to relax."

"Well, that's what I always say. Can I get you a cup of coffee to start?"

"Do you have any iced tea?"

Stella looked shocked. "Iced tea. Iced tea. Well, let me think about that. I'll tell you what. We can make you some *tea* and give you a glass with *ice cubes* in it. That suit you?"

"Sounds great." Stella trundled off, her slightly bowed legs rolling as rapidly as if she were riding a unicycle.

"Iced tea! Dwight, what are you thinking of?"

"Don't you get tired of coffee sometimes?"

"You could have ordered a Pepsi."

"All they serve here is that blasted Kik Cola. Try to pass it off as the real thing."

"You're putting Stella to a lot of trouble."

"All she has to do is make two pots of tea and give us some ice cubes."

"Honestly."

Salem Alderman hove into view, his generous belly in full billow, a genial smile plastered across his broad face.

"Well, folks. You must be pretty excited."

"Excited?" Sadie said defensively.

"My, yes. And it's only a couple of months away."

"What is?"

"Don't tell me you don't know!"

"Know what?"

"About the reunion for Min's birthday. You mean to say Eileen hasn't even told you? Everybody in town must know by now."

"Dwight! Why didn't you say something?"

His face was turning a funny colour, several colours at once in fact. It almost matched the plaid of his shirt.

"I was meaning to break it to you tonight," he said, raising his eyebrows in an innocent look that he hoped would placate her. It used to work on Min.

"Does this mean you'll have to talk to—"

"Looks like it. Or at least see him. Maybe it's time we put this whole thing behind us, anyway."

"Good for you, Dwight," bellowed Salem, embarrassing Sadie acutely. "Bury the hatchet. That's what I always say."

"What does Barlow think?"

"Barlow's Barlow. He doesn't tell me what he thinks."

"Barlow's a grand chap." Sadie gave him a look, but it had no effect. To Salem it was the same mild, neutral look she always wore. But they were trying to have a private conversation here. Salem was about as subtle as a hunk of bologna, not taking the hint.

"Gosh, I'm thirsty in this heat. Could you get us a glass of water, Sale?" A stroke of genius. At once Sadie remembered why she had married Dwight. He was good at handling awkward moments. He always found a way for them to grease their way through.

"Thank you, dear."

"Aw, Sade. I was going to tell you about it."

"Never mind. Your mother's not getting any younger. Maybe this way the family will at least be speaking to each other at her memorial."

"She's not dead yet."

"I didn't say she was."

"They're going to have it in Gribble Park."

"At the park? There's too many hippies hanging around."

"Sade. They're just kids. Decent kids, too. Their parents wouldn't let them get away with anything bad."

"Have you seen how they dress?"

"They just want to keep up with the latest styles." Dwight was starting to feel a little warm in his madras plaid shirt.

"But they take drugs."

"Oh, they only smoke a little pot."

"You make it sound like nothing. Like drinking a beer."

Dwight knew he wasn't going to win this one.

"The kids won't be a problem. They'll blend right in. Eileen says they're going to pitch a big tent and serve Colonel Sanders."

"Colonel Sanders! Doesn't she realize what that'll cost?"

"There'll be games for the kiddies, jugglers, balloons, the Harman Kiltie Band, the whole works."

"Sounds like a circus."

Stella hurtled towards them with two teapots and two glasses of ice cubes on a tray. She slammed it down cheerfully between them.

"Iced tea," she announced.

Dwight poured steaming tea into a glass. The ice cracked, groaned and shrivelled away to almost nothing. Sadie looked down at her tea as if it were a noxious substance. Warm brown fluid with a skin of tannin on top.

"It wouldn't hurt you to try it," Dwight said in a slightly seductive voice.

Turning on his best little-boy smile, he reached across the table and clinked his glass of iced tea against hers.

9.

Bob Hemphill sat in the living room of the old Gribble place with a cigarette in one hand and a cup of coffee in the other. He gazed out the large picture window at chestnut trees bubbling with blossom, their creamy, heaped-up blooms looking good enough to eat. Beside him, a tiny grey tabby kitten with the fuzzy, embryonic look of a baby bird batted at a stray thread on the sofa, grey felt ears vigorously perked forward into points. Bob smiled. He had always felt a certain affinity for animals.

Agnes hadn't known what to think when Shelton brought this strange young man home with him, "just for a little while, until he gets his bearings." For her, it all came down to more meals prepared, shirts and bed linens washed, and extra cases of beer brought in. And how long was a "little while" supposed to mean, anyway, when that Mordecai fellow had stayed on for more than a month? The Glenfiddich hadn't been good enough for him, either. He'd insisted Shelton go out and buy Glenlivet. Glen this, Glen that—wasn't one just as good as the other?

This new one, this Bob, looked like a hippie —though she'd say this much about him, he was clean. Well-spoken, too, as if he'd had an education or at least read a lot of books. Not everyone Shelton brought home was that refined. He once got drunk with a gimpy old Cree named Joseph Half Leg and let him stay for weeks, picking his brain for stories of his people's vanishing way of life. Agnes suspected Shelton did this—capturing live specimens and studying them until he got tired of them—as a strange form of research for his books. Rather than go out and perform all the tiresome rituals of living, he found representatives of life to bring back home with him, to save himself the trouble. Once he had pretty much sucked them dry of their vital force, they were free to leave.

But how was Agnes supposed to understand the mind of a writer anyway? Her job was to free Shelton from responsibility for a myriad of tedious daily tasks—the shopping, cooking, cleaning, driving the car, even typing his manuscripts—so that he could get on with his writing and not have to bother himself with anything else. And then there was the sex. She chided herself for adding it to the list of chores, but lately it was about as enjoyable as doing the ironing. One more thing to cross off before she could sleep. Shelton was well into his seventies and you'd think he'd be past all that, but his appetites surfaced as regularly as his requirement for clean shirts and wholesome food.

What melted Agnes's resistance to this new fellow, this Bob, was an episode she was calling the Miracle of the Muffin. It had taken her years to persuade Shelton to allow a cat in the house, and even at that he only tolerated wee Muffie, pretending to step on her when she was asleep. On Bob's first night at the Gribble place, he and Shelton were deeply engaged in conversation about something called Eckankar (and as usual Agnes had no idea what they were talking about, just kept serving the coffee when their cups were empty), when they heard a feral-sounding, snarling hiss coming from the kitchen. Agnes got there just as the borzoi Ranulf was letting the tiny grey blob of fur drop from his jaws. The skinny hound cowered down to the floor, dribbling a trail of urine as Agnes swatted him across the behind, then shot out of the room to go hide under his master's bed. Muffin lay there inert, boneless, her back apparently broken, as Agnes wailed, "My baby! My sweet little baby girl!"

At the sound of anguish in her voice, Bob rushed in to the kitchen and knelt on the floor beside the dead kitten.

"That monster," Agnes blubbered, "he picked that sweet little thing up in his jaws and just shook her. My poor little lamb."

"Let me see her." Bob tenderly scooped up the limp body, which he could easily cradle in one hand, then brought it up to his face. He appeared to be breathing on her. Agnes watched in rapt and somewhat frightened fascination.

For a long moment he held her, covering her broken body with his other hand. Agnes felt a sort of heat in the room, but not the kind of heat you feel from a fireplace. Another kind. She didn't want to think of what it reminded her of. A crazy old lady she knew who used to do "laying on of hands" in a church basement full of hysterical fundamentalists. But this was quieter, steadier, no theatrics at all. No shouts of hallelujah. Just a luminous, invisible heat. The kitten's sides heaved and she opened her eyes and mewed. Bob set her carefully down, and she shook herself and began washing her face.

"What did you do?" Agnes breathed, turning pale.

Shelton stood in the doorway. "She was just stunned. Nothing wrong with her, really."

"Yeah, you're probably right," Bob said, getting up off the floor.

Now Agnes observed Bob on the sofa with Muffin, her baby girl returned from the dead. It was a little unusual to watch Jesus smoking a cigarette, but that's exactly what it looked like.

"Do you go to church?" The question startled him a little. He turned around and smiled up at her shyly.

"Haven't for a long time. We were Lutherans. I thought it was all a little stuffy. I feel closest to God when I'm out in the bush."

"Shelton's an atheist. Or at least he says he is. Sometimes I wonder about that."

"Maybe God believes in him." Agnes thought that was just about the most wonderful thing she had ever heard. Her love was now complete, and she hoped Bob would stay with them forever.

"Oh Bob, that's so—so spiritual."

"It's hard to believe we came out of nothing," Bob said, taking a drag. The kitten suddenly scrambled up his body as if it were a tree trunk, and he laughed.

"Animals know."

"They're God's creatures. Aren't you, Muffin? You're the apple of God's eye."

"You should write."

"I've tried it. Percy writes, doesn't he?"

"He hasn't told you yet? Oh well, you'll find out."

"I noticed a whole shelf of books by the same author. The publication dates were in chronological order. I wondered."

"You're very observant."

"So should I call him Shelton now?"

"Everyone else does."

"Writers are interesting." Muffin was now lying sprawled on top of Bob's head. For some reason it didn't look silly.

Shelton came in in his old bathrobe with a cup of coffee, looking crumpled and grey as he always did first thing in the morning. The latest book hadn't been going well; Agnes could tell by his testy mood. Maybe he was getting tired of moving the same characters around on the mental chessboard for volume after volume. Maybe it was uncharitable of Agnes to think so—after all, what did she know about literature? But she wondered if Shelton ever got tired of spewing out the same sort of novel year after year. It was getting so that Elmsdale was less interesting than Harman (though it was a damn sight better than Horgansville). Once everyone's clothes are off, how much farther can you go?

He was angling for something fresh, Agnes knew. There was purpose and pattern in his bringing Bob home with him, just as there was calculation behind every single thing he ever did.

"Well, Bob," said Shelton. "Are you going to tell me about this mission of yours?"

"Mission?" Bob looked startled and innocent. Agnes could see Shelton moving in for the kill. There was a mystery here, marrow to be sucked.

"When we met in the bakery, you said to me, 'You might say I'm on a mission.'"

"So I did." A sort of veil came down over Bob's Christly face, and Shelton knew he'd have to try a little harder.

"Is it a religious thing?"

"Not exactly. More like . . . an identity thing."

"Finding out who you are?"

"My roots."

"D'you have family here?" Agnes noticed Bob was looking a little uncomfortable. Shelton was awfully good at figuring things out, like a detective.

"I'm not sure yet." He stubbed out his cigarette, not wanting to meet Shelton's eyes.

A lion knows enough to withdraw behind the bushes when its prey gets nervous. Pull back, create an illusion of calm.

"Agnes, run and get us some more coffee, will you? There's a dear. Bob, would you like some eggs?"

"No, thanks. I don't usually eat breakfast."

"Not fasting, are you?"

"I'm not Gandhi."

"But you're a fine young man, Bob. Intelligent, discerning. A diamond in a sea of stones."

"You don't know me very well, Percy. Or should I say Shelton."

"So my secret is out."

"I sort of figured it out from your bookshelves. Seventeen novels—that's quite an accomplishment."

"Have you read any of them?"

"I'm afraid I haven't had the pleasure."

"My work doesn't usually appeal to your age group. The kids aren't easily shocked. Over-forties, though—they can't get enough of it. My characters do all the things they wish they could get away with."

Agnes came in with coffee and day-old Danish pastries from Guy's. Shelton looked slightly disapproving. Store-bought. Bob leaned forward enthusiastically and took one, "Thanks, Agnes. These look great." Agnes was positively glowing. Probably has a crush on him, Shelton thought sourly. It was hard to get a rise out of her these days. All the usual tricks didn't work. Was she after someone younger? Something with firmer flesh? But lusting after Jesus just seemed indecent.

"What sort of work do you do, Bob?" Agnes asked sweetly.

"Oh, this and that. Day labour, mostly. I dropped out of university in Edmonton last year."

"Edmonton?" *Who did he know in Edmonton?*

"It wasn't my thing. I figured there were other ways to expand my mind."

"Not those funny mushrooms?"

"No, not drugs. They're just a cheap high. I mean— travel. Engaging with people."

"So you earn just enough to keep yourself going."

"So far." He lit another cigarette. "Then there's my poetry."

"Poetry!" *Now we're getting to it*, Shelton thought.

"It's not much. I'm not up to the standard of my heroes—Dylan, Cohen."

"I know Dylan Thomas, but who's Cohen?"

Bob burst out laughing, then turned a little red.

"I'm sorry. I meant that other Dylan—Bob. 'He not busy born is busy dying.' And Leonard Cohen—'Oh, the sisters of mercy, they are not departed or gone—'"

"Oh, your voice is lovely," Agnes quavered.

"Can't say as I've heard of him. Though that Dylan fellow, didn't he write 'Blowin' in the Wind'?"

"That, and a host of others. 'Hey, Mr. Tambourine Man, play a song for me . . . in the jingle-jangle mornin', I'll come followin' you.'"

At the sound of his voice, Agnes's eyes shone with rapture. Shelton noticed this. He'd seen that look before, in their early days, back when things were still sweet in the bedroom.

"Well, it's not all bad. This young stuff. Alan Ginsberg wrote a few good ones. You have to keep your mind open."

"It helps."

"So what are your plans for today, Bob?"

"Thought I'd go look for work."

"Too early for the tobacco crop."

"I'll find something. Fruit-picking, digging a ditch."

"Man's work," Agnes breathed. Shelton wondered what she was implying.

"I appreciate your generosity in putting me up," Bob said, "but I'll be finding a place of my own as soon as I can."

"No hurry. We enjoy your company."

"I'd like to repay you."

"No need. It'd be an honour if I can help you complete your mission."

"It's a private one."

"But those are the best kind." Shelton had found his way in, and wasn't going to lose ground now. "Friends are here to help each other, aren't they?"

Suddenly, unexpectedly, a shock to all three of them, tears formed in Bob's heartbreakingly blue eyes. Agnes thought he looked unbearably lonely and vulnerable. She wanted to bury his face between her breasts. Even Shelton felt touched.

"I don't know how to thank you," Bob said in a faltering voice. "I've come a long, long way."

Shelton leaned towards him, his seamed face a study in enigma. "Welcome home," he said.

10.

Aubrey was feeling remarkably chipper these days, the way you feel after the worst has already happened. Once the dust had settled from the major trauma of Min's announcement, life fell back into its accustomed groove. Aubrey and Pearl drove to Toronto to attend a grand performance of *Rigoletto*, and no, Min didn't fall down and break her hip while they were away. He'd had no more letters from illegitimate sons, no more phone calls from phantom siblings. The days kept passing, the usual round of Pep flakes and chicken dinners with cabbage salad, and picking up day-old bread at the bakery to save a few cents.

"Mrs. McConnaughey. And how might you be on this fine day?"

"Aubrey. My, you're looking cheerful. Any special reason?"

"No major disasters this week. Can't complain. Two loaves of potato bread from the sale bin, Guy. And wrap us up a couple of spudnuts. Give me the chocolate this time."

"You never buy chocolate." Guy looked a little concerned.

"This is the *new* Aubrey," Ethel McConnaughey twittered. Her cheeks were so furred with face powder she resembled a pollen-dusted bumblebee in the summer sunshine.

"We're tired of the pink," Aubrey said.

"They're cerise," Ethel corrected. The hue closely matched her twin blooms of peony-coloured rouge.

"Whatever they are, we'd like a change."

"And how's Min, the old dear? Full of excitement about the reunion?"

"It's given her something to occupy her time," he admitted. Since nothing traumatic had happened for a couple of weeks, he was beginning to feel the reunion might not be the ordeal he had anticipated. No worse than going to the dentist, or being poked with a sharp stick.

"I can get you a clown," Ethel said. "He doesn't charge the earth like these city clowns. Blows up those long, thin balloons and makes animals out of them."

Ye gods! Aubrey knew who she was talking about. Ethel's cousin Hank Ritter held the record for the highest number of slips in his AA group. He was a disaster on legs who had never put together more than ten days of sobriety in a row.

"You don't mean Happy Hank?" *The piss-tank,* Aubrey mentally added.

"Now, Aubrey. Give him a chance. What if people hadn't allowed you to rehabilitate yourself?"

Jesus, Aubrey thought. Happy Hank had been banned from clowning a couple of years ago for appearing inebriated at Randy Jamieson's sixth birthday party. Things went along well enough at first, except for some of the kiddies complaining about the fumes. Then he twisted a balloon into a shape which struck Eunice Sanderson, the minister's wife, as highly suggestive, if not downright obscene. "It was supposed to be a dachshund!" Hank protested. What sort of a dirty mind would see a frankly phallic shape in an innocent little dog? But Hank had forgotten to put on the hind legs. Then when he threw up into a cardboard box containing a brand new Meccano set, the jig was up. Happy Hank was given the bum's rush out the door as Ninian Sanderson tried to resurrect some of his dusty old magic tricks from his college days. He pulled a fifty-cent piece out of young Randy's ear, and the ungrateful snot snatched it out of his hand and put it in his pocket. "It came out of *my* ear," he said sullenly. "I'm keeping it."

"I don't think we'll be needing a clown," Aubrey said uncomfortably. Then the doorbell dinged and Agnes Flood bustled in, looking radiant to the point of mania.

"Good morning, Guy. Aubrey. Ethel. Oh, what a beautiful morning!" Aubrey prayed she wouldn't begin to sing.

"My, my," Ethel said. "Aren't we cheerful today."

"Four loaves of cracked wheat, Guy."

"*Four?*" Ethel clearly disapproved of this extravagance.

"We have a guest."

"Oh! The young man!" Ethel pinkened at the memory of seeing the image of her Saviour eating a doughnut in this very room.

"What young man?" Aubrey asked.

"Oh, he's wonderful. His name is Bob and he's a poet. He brought Muffin back from the dead."

"He *what?*"

"My kitty. She died when Shelton's horrible dog broke her back. But Bob just took her up in his hands and blessed her, and—"

"Agnes. Aren't you getting a little bit carried away?" Aubrey thought the woman was raving. But Ethel looked fascinated.

"He healed your cat?" she breathed, her eyes shining.

"Shelton thinks it was just a coincidence. But I know better. Aubrey, you *have* to meet him."

"Is he the one with the long hair?" Soapy had mentioned seeing another one of them damn hippies, a new one this time, as if this town needed any more of those. "It's them damn Beatles, them asses," he had fumed. Soapy believed that society's decline and fall could be traced back to February 9, 1964, when the Beatles made their first appearance on the Ed Sullivan Show amid the plate-spinners and the contortionists. As if Sophie Tucker and Topo Gigio weren't enough of an entertainment for decent folks.

"Yes, but it's—"

"Clean?" Aubrey said.

"How did you know what I was going to say?"

"Call it a good guess. Well, good luck with your guest. I'll have to be going now." He clanged out the door.

"He seems happy," Ethel said doubtfully.

"Oh, Ethel. Don't be so suspicious."

"What's bred in the bone will come out in the flesh," she pronounced, thinking of Melville Connar's legendary boozing sprees.

"Maybe he's just happy about the reunion."

"Happy my foot. He can't stand his brothers. And that poor Eileen."

"Is she that great big woman with the—"

"Yes, she's the one with the—" Ethel gestured widely in front of her chest.

"And is she the one with all the—you know—"

"Well, I lost count of her husbands after number five." The two of them cackled with laughter. Behind the counter, Guy winced.

Guy heard lots of things. He could have been the

town psychiatrist, if Harman had ever needed such a thing. People confessed to him all the time, as if he were a bartender or a priest. Even serious things, like adultery. Guy didn't know what to do except keep on pouring coffee. It was his ministry.

"They say it'll have an Irish theme," said Ethel, her mouth a little pursed.

"I didn't realize they were—"

"They aren't. Not properly, anyway. Do you know what Dan Ryerson said the other day? 'The Connars are Irish like Harland Sanders is a colonel.'" This set the two of them off into gales of laughter again. Guy wondered for the thousandth time why they had to laugh at other people's expense.

"I've heard stories about old Uncle Whit," Agnes said, egging Ethel on.

"Whit was mentally disturbed. He should have been in an institution. It was his radio, you know."

"What radio?"

"The one Aubrey still listens to. I'm amazed he can get it to work at all. Of course, I don't believe the rumours for a minute, but I've heard he can get Vic and Sade on that thing."

"Vic and—"

"You're too young to remember, dear. Old Ben Gambert went over there late one night when the toilet overflowed, way after hours, but then he and Aubrey are friends from way back. As he was fixing the toilet he could have sworn he heard Vic and Sade playing on that radio, but when he came into the parlour it was only the late news broadcast on the CBC."

"Didn't there used to be a dog in the house?"

"Don't get me started on that dog. Probably a health hazard. Do you know that it had to be put down for biting Nin Sanderson's poor old halfwit of a father, Thaddeus?"

"Ladies," Guy said as cheerfully as he could while grinding his back teeth. "Won't you sit down and have a cup of coffee? It's on the house."

They both oohed and twittered as he escorted them to their table, hoping this intervention would stem the flow of gabble for a while. But it was all in vain. They sat with their heads close together, their eyes sparkling as they dissected the legendary Connar eccentricities. Guy sighed, hearing their voices rise and fall, catching the tone if not the words.

Agnes looked at her watch and jumped. "Oh! I have to be going. Bob will want his lunch. He only eats wholegrain bread, you know."

"Does he."

"Yes, and you should hear him sing. Just like Glen Campbell."

"I'm sure."

"I'll see you later, Ethel." She bustled out, practically trailing radiance.

Ethel sipped her coffee for a moment, then looked up at Guy.

"Nice sort of girl, that Agnes. She has a good heart. Too bad she's living in sin."

"Writers," Guy said, hoping that would explain it all. He got her the usual order of two white loaves and a small bag of thimble cookies—the ones with the red jam in the centre that Evan liked—without even asking her what she wanted. This seemed to please her.

Ethel walked with her clipped, spindle-heeled steps

past Aubrey's house, wondering if she should drop in on Min. Then thought better of it—she could swear she always smelled urine in that house, though maybe it was only the stale reminder of corned beef and cabbage. What Agnes had told her was stroking her thoughts like harp strings. The young man did have a certain . . . presence. And then there was Muffin. True, maybe the kitten hadn't exactly come back from the dead, but can anyone be sure about these things? Ethel had once gone to a revival service without telling anybody—she prayed she wouldn't run into anyone she knew—and saw a man healed of his deafness just by having his head pushed over backwards.

It had been a long time since Evan had walked. His arthritis was slowly, relentlessly taking over his body, one joint after another, first licking at his bones in all sorts of subtle and sadistic ways, then landing in with a vengeance after his retirement. Now he was just a bent-over, shrivelled shell of himself. Ethel couldn't get him to eat properly at all. All he seemed to want were things like creamed chipped beef on toast, Junket pudding, and store-bought cookies. Invalid food. Helping him use the bathroom was a nightmare. Ethel had a part-time nurse come in for things like bathing. But it was almost like not having a husband at all. At times she was deeply ashamed to find herself sharply envious of the town widows, going off for jolly vacations in France and taking up with new companions while their children watched in horror.

No, it wasn't as if she wanted Evan dead. She just wanted him able-bodied again, capable of putting on the storm windows in the fall and mowing the front lawn so she wouldn't have to have a boy in to do it. And maybe capable of a conversation that didn't always revolve around how much pain he was in. Ethel wondered if she should talk to this Bob. Certainly the doctors had been of no help at all: "Well, Ethel, it's just his age, you know," though Evan was all of sixty-seven and his father had lived to be nearly ninety.

She remembered the swampy, steamy atmosphere in the revival tent, the preacher with the soaked armpits and auctioneer's voice haranguing them all for their sins and commanding them to turn to *"Jeeeee-zus,"* which he pronounced like the braying of a mule. She blushed as she remembered him calling all the sinners to the front for public repentance, and the way she had climbed to her feet as if by remote control and taken one shaky step at a time until she was actually standing there at the front, shoulder to shoulder with the weeping, sweating crowd. The revivalist smelled bad, rank body odour mixed with something else. He lurched towards her, pushing her forehead in a sharp smack of blessing, and to her horror Ethel had a sort of convulsion, an indecent sensation that she couldn't begin to explain. Her knees had buckled and she began to sob in a loud voice, "Yes! Yes! Yes!" while the preacher knelt beside her, spitting out "Praise the name of Jesus" like a vindictive curse. When she got home that night, deeply humiliated by her loss of control, her underpants were soaked, just like an incontinent old woman. Or worse.

She never went back, but a certain flame of yearning had been lit in her breast and could never be extinguished. As unlikely as it seemed, Ethel McConnaughey the incorrigible town gossip had a taste for miracles. Perhaps she should invite this interesting young man over for tea.

11.

In Horgansville, during the sweet virgin days of summer, after a scorcher of a day when the cicadas had buzzed up a storm, there was a place you could go to cool down and refresh yourself. You could bring the kiddies and Grandma and Uncle Gerald and even your cousin Mervin who wasn't right in the head, and nobody minded. It was called the Peerless, and it was a community ritual to gather there for a treat, as much a part of the season as the hypnotic singing of cicadas, peeling skin, and insect bites.

Even Stella and Salem, who were seldom off-duty at the Fry King, came to the Peerless on a summer evening after closing time to get away from the heat, the grease, and the flies. Stella was fond of floats, whereas Salem always had the same thing, a strawberry malt with an egg in it, with a glass of ice water on the side.

But you didn't just go to the Peerless Dairy Bar for the top-notch refreshments. You went for the talk. Ten minutes at the Peerless would catch you up on all of the latest better than an hour in that ungodly bakery in Harman, which was run by a foreigner, so what could you expect? When Stella and Salem heaved their considerable bulk into a booth opposite Sara Ray and Barlow Connar, it didn't take long for them to be brought up to speed.

Stella was regaling them all with a story about the rat-sized chihuahua she used to have that kept wandering out into the street.

"'Tiny,' I said to him, 'don't you do that, you bad little dog. One day you're going to be hit by a car.' And do you know what happened one day?"

"He was hit by a car," said Sara Ray in her flat matter-of-fact voice.

"Yes, hit by a car. Hit by a car, just like I said. And do you know what happened to that dog?"

"I think they've heard this story before, dear," Salem said, but Stella ploughed on.

"That little dog, that Tiny, he just flew up into the air, then came down and hit the pavement. You know what happened next?"

"Tell me," said Sara Ray, who knew every word of this story.

"He bounced. That Tiny, that wee little dog, he bounced. Not once, but twice, like one of them Superballs the kids play with. Bounced like he was made out of India rubber."

"What happened next?" Barlow asked.

"Well, you know, that little dog just got up, shook himself, and came trotting right over to me, wagging his tail as if nothing had happened."

"That sure was a tough little dog," said Barlow, as if on cue.

"Tough little dog. Tough little dog. How's your sundae, Sara Ray?"

"It's good. How's your Moonglow?" It was a special concoction made from ginger ale and orange sherbet, which Stella insisted on pronouncing "sherbert."

"Dreamy, thanks. But that Tiny. Tough little dog."

"Tough little dog," Barlow agreed, praying the story would end soon. Then he saw to his relief that Herb Ritter, face as florid as a tomato, was bearing down on them full-tilt. He leaned over and pounded on the table.

"So, folks! Are you coming to Horgie Days?"

"Horgie Days. Herb, we haven't had Horgie Days in about fifteen years," Stella said, lighting an Export A.

"All the more reason to come, my dear. We're bringing it back, and I think it's high time, too."

"When's it on? Not the middle of August like it used to be?"

"Of course it is. It's a tradition."

"But that's the same time as—"

"The reunion," Sara Ray said to Barlow. For one sweet second, hope flared like the beam of a searchlight in his imagination. Perhaps this would give him an "out."

"Reunion, shree-union. We've got better things to do than celebrate some old lady's birthday." Herb suddenly realized what he had said. "Sorry, Barl. I admire old Min. And you're only ninety once. But this town needs an event of its own. So we're having a three-day celebration called Horgansville Pride Days. A big parade with floats, games, a wiener roast, entertainment—"

"Not your brother," Sara Ray said flatly.

"Hank's a changed man, Sara Ray. Hasn't touched the stuff in a year."

"That's not what I heard." Sara Ray got away with a lot because she spoke so softly, you weren't sure what she had said.

"But doesn't that mean that folks will have to decide which event to go to?" Stella asked, the inverted V's of her eyebrows puckering together.

"Half of Horgansville is going to Min's birthday," Salem threw in, noisily sucking up the viscous pink dregs of his malt. It reminded Sara Ray of a baby goat nursing on a nanny's tit.

"We'll just have to advertise. A big spread in the Horgansville Bugler. Posters everywhere. It's time we revived the spirit of this place. Show the rest of Fulford County what we're made of."

"And show Harman what a two-bit backwater it is," Barlow chuckled, looking pleased.

"Barlow! What would your mother say?" Sara Ray hissed, then tried to suppress a smirk. She imagined for a moment the wicked fun of snubbing her own mother-in-law, getting back at her for that Pope's nose remark at the wedding.

"Of course you folks have family loyalties to consider. But I expect everybody else in town to come out to Horgie Days. Did you hear that, folks?" Herb bellowed, loudly enough so that no one in the Peerless could ignore him. Sara Ray looked mortified. "August thirteenth to the fifteenth. Mark it on your calendars. It's Horgie Days!" Most of the patrons looked confused, and a vindictive-looking five-year-old hurled a cherry at Herb, which hit him and bounced off his forehead. Herb grinned back at the little tyke, wiping melted ice cream off his face with a handkerchief as the kid's mother shrieked, "Davy!" and swatted him.

"David and Goliath," Salem said under his breath, and the four of them at the table wheezed with suppressed laughter. Herb, incapable of being in on a joke on himself, kept grinning like a crazed jack-o'-lantern, showing all his silver bridgework.

He was gaping like this when Eileen Connar burst through the door and strode up to the counter, wearing a lime-green crimpolene pantsuit with bell-bottomed slacks that hugged her round behind. The smile took on just the hint of a leer. "Eileen!" he boomed.

"Herb." Close behind Eileen trailed her youngest daughter Bernadette, tall and freckly and gangly as a fawn, her sticklike body swelling at the belly with an incongruous-looking pregnancy.

"My, will you look at that," Stella murmured.

"No guidance at all," Sara Ray mumbled.

"Well, just look at her mother. What's her last name these days anyway?"

"She's gone back to Connar," Sara Ray muttered, "to reduce the confusion."

With great dignity, Eileen ordered two hot fudge sundaes with "redskin" peanuts, rising above the vindictive buzzing in various parts of the room. Even the men looked at each other and said things like, "Too bad." Some of them noted Eileen's monumental breasts.

"Now you eat this," Eileen said to Bernadette, who was peering nervously around, aware on some level of the social disapproval hanging in the air like an odour. Eileen was such an old hand at managing disapproval that she wore it lightly, like a loose garment. But this was Bernadette's first trip to purgatory, and the subtle static of the town's moral rejection affected her keenly.

"Oh, Mother."

"You're not eating enough. And none of it has any food value." Eileen had posted Canada's Food Rules on the fridge at home, but so far it had had no effect. "Mother," she moaned. "It says I have to have *ten* servings of vegetables a day." Bernadette continued to live on a diet of Cherry Blossoms, sour-cream-and-onion chips, and Squirt.

"Eat up. Ice cream is so wholesome," Eileen sighed, dipping into her own treat with a little shiver of pleasure.

She still wasn't sure what the arrangement would be when the baby was born in the fall. At first Bernadette had wanted to get married. Seismic memories of Eileen's forced first marriage heaved up from the bedrock of her subconscious, and she begged her daughter not to. Bernadette wasn't too sure which of her boyfriends was the father, but she did have a favourite, Donny, so mild and gentle it was hard for Eileen to imagine him having sexual relations with anyone. He seemed to think having a baby was sort of like getting a puppy. Come to think of it, Eileen thought, it is. Surely looking after a dog is a lot more like raising a baby than playing with an inanimate chunk of plastic wearing booties.

"I'm not going back to school in the fall," Bernadette said calmly, chasing peanuts around in the sundae dish and eating practically nothing.

"Not going back to school! What do you mean? I thought it was understood that you—"

"I want to look after the baby. You've got your real-estate job to think about, Mother."

"I can switch to part-time. I can manage."

"But aren't you a little tired of babies?" Bernadette had her there. After eleven of them, with Bernadette the last now at age fifteen, Eileen was indeed weary of the whole process. Soon her youngest son Ronan would be leaving home to go to trade school. She'd been looking forward to life with just the two of them. No—make that three.

Eileen thought of the baby—in her mind's eye she saw a ginger-haired, freckle-dusted little girl wearing gingham—and her heart began to melt like the goo in Bernadette's dish. But it was such a long job. Eileen had been a mother since—when was it, 1932? She didn't want to total up the years. Much more than half her life, with no freedom in sight.

Or maybe it would be twins. Min had Barlow and Dwight, after all, and breast-fed them for a year. Eileen felt a headache coming on.

"I'd like to call him Sebastian. After that guy in the Lovin' Spoonful."

"What sort of name is that? It's not even Irish." Eileen, who was partial to names like Finbarr and Mavourneen, was shocked.

"Neither are we, Mother. Or Grace, for a girl. You know— 'Don't you want somebody to love, don't you need somebody to love—'"

"No, I don't know. What are you talking about?"

"Mother. You're so uncool."

"Was it being 'cool' that brought you to this state, then?" Eileen could hear Min's shrill tone echoing in her own voice: "Stand up straight. Merciful God, girl. How far gone are you?" The last thing Eileen had ever wanted was to sound like her mother.

For that matter, she had wanted even less for Bernadette to follow in her wayward footsteps. She'd always intended to have "the talk" with her, to explain things about boys and sex, and somehow it just never came about. Min's tight-lipped, mortified face had rendered the subject completely taboo.

So instead of wisdom and knowledge, she ended up

passing along silence, discomfort, shame, and—finally—the same fatal ignorance that had landed her in a loveless marriage with a homosexual.

Bernadette must have been reading her thoughts. She levelled her gaze at her mother. "At least I'm not marrying a queer."

It was a direct hit. Eileen was stung to the quick. "Mind your mouth, young lady," she shot back, trying to suppress the quiver in her lower lip.

Why, why, oh why? Why, when we love each other more than life itself, do we do and say such nasty things to each other? It was the Connar curse, Eileen supposed, a disease that afflicted the whole family like a congenital plague.

"Sorry, Mother," Bernadette said glumly, feeling a pang of guilt at Eileen's suddenly red-rimmed eyes. "Queers aren't so bad. Look at Shelby."

"Shelby's a fine young man," Eileen sniffed, trying hard to regain her composure.

"But a queer. Or should I say, he does his own thing, which in his case means boys."

"Bernadette."

"Well, it's true. I wonder if I'll ever see him again."

"Toronto's not the moon. Why don't you write to him?"

"He's the big brother. S'posed to be the responsible one."

"I wish he weren't so far away." Shelby was approaching middle age now, and Eileen hardly knew him. She yearned for him to come to the reunion, but wouldn't let herself hope. It wasn't as if the rest of the family had cut him off. He'd cut himself off. She knew he was different.

So had Shelton been different, but in such a lovely way. So sensitive. Sometimes she wondered if Shelby had somehow absorbed his difference from Robbie, though she doubted such a thing was possible. Robbie had tried to be a good husband, was a good provider (and in those days, that particular trait went far), but he just didn't love her. After a few years of life together, he didn't even like her. It was one of the quiet tragedies that people live with all the time. After less than five years, they had parted. How could Shelby have absorbed his stepfather's queerness in such a short time when there was no sign of it at home?

"Anyway, he's coming to the reunion," Eileen said, forcing brightness into her tone.

"You hope."

"Yes, I do hope."

"Will he bring Greg?" She pronounced the name as if Greg were a different species.

"He can bring anyone he likes. He's my son."

"So why can't I bring Donny?"

"Let's not start on that again. Besides, it's such a long way off. Can't we just enjoy the summer?"

"Not so long. Only a few more weeks." Bernadette finally took a bite of her sundae. "My God. By then I'll be just about ready to pop."

"Bernadette. Such expressions." For a moment Eileen frowned, but then the lines on her face all reversed themselves and she giggled like a girl. Bernadette looked up at her in surprise, then laughed. The two of them looked directly into each other's eyes, and you could have sworn they were physically joined, fastened together almost visibly by a bright beam of love.

12.

Eileen sat in her housecoat at the kitchen table of the tidy apartment she shared with Ronan and Bernadette, leafing listlessly through the *Bugler*, which seemed to be mostly ads for Horgie Days, which she was already sick of hearing about. She thought of yesterday's brief encounter at the Peerless with Herb Ritter, and wondered if anyone had noticed the brightening of his eye when she walked in the door. The truth of it was she was seeing Herb, but trying to keep it a secret (about as likely as Min Connar winning a beauty contest, in this place).

Eileen had always been able to steel herself against the murmurings of a small town, but at this point in her life, with Bernadette expecting and all, she had no wish to further loam the fertile fields of gossip. Herb had only been widowed for a couple of months, and it wouldn't sit well with the townsfolk that he seemed so prematurely hot to trot. There was more to it than that, of course; Herb had started seeing Eileen some months before Edna had died of a particularly vicious form of pelvic cancer. The man was in need of comfort. As usual, Eileen strove to be as discreet as possible.

For this was an affair, plain and simple, and Eileen hadn't really had one of those since her ill-fated romance with Shelton all those years ago. Eileen knew she didn't love Herb—in fact, frankly, he irritated her with his booming voice, overbearingly bluff manner, and perpetually shiny forehead. He always seemed to be oozing with the glistening grease of enthusiasm. But Herb, unlikely as it seemed, knew a thing or two about pleasuring a female body. He wasn't squeamish about odours or sounds or secretions; in fact, his appreciation for all the wonders of Eileen's mature body knew no bounds. Not since Shelton had introduced her to the sublime pleasures of something he called *cunnilingus* (which was all too quickly taken away again for over thirty years) had she felt such deep gratification.

This was a surprise to her. Once she had gone through the change, she'd figured that was that, the end of her sexual viability. When Herb proved her wrong, Eileen began to feel as kittenish as a young girl. Why not? Though the chassis was bulkier and less flexible, everything still worked.

In a pensive mood, Eileen took down the old green leather-bound autograph book from the top shelf of her bookcase, and it fell open in the middle, releasing an odour of mellow old paper that triggered a surge of memory. Autograph books, like virginity in young women, had gone the way of the dinosaur in recent times, but Eileen remembered collecting the little verses, homilies, and signatures from her school chums as a keepsake, with no idea of how much things would change in the coming years.

"A maid, a man,
A dainty fan,
A seat upon the stair.
A word, a kiss,
Two weeks of bliss,

Then forty years of care.

Beware!"

This little ditty was signed by Howie Hudson, not yet nicknamed Soapy, and with no idea that he'd end up marrying Eileen years and years later. She supposed she should have taken the cynical verse as a warning.

Russell Mudge had written, "Thanks for all the good times, Leenie," embarrassing her thoroughly. After all, all they'd done was kiss once at the movies, a Harry Langdon comedy, she seemed to recall. Trying to keep her eye on the baby-faced, backward comedian's awkward antics, she hadn't been at all prepared for the aggressive thrustings of Russell's tongue, something you never saw in the movies. Kisses were supposed to be prolonged and passionate, but not slimy. Rudolph Valentino, whom Russell called "that pansy," never used his tongue.

Then came the verse that she cherished the most. It still had the power to quicken her pulse.

"How many loved your moments of glad grace

And loved your beauty with love false or true,

But one man loved the pilgrim soul in you,

And loved the sorrows of your changing face."

Eileen thought that this was the most beautiful thing she had ever read. It was signed "Your Secret Amour" in Shelton's graceful, sloping hand, the special one he used at his book signings, which bore no relation to his tilting, jagged first-draft scrawl.

Eileen had been contemplating writing to Shelton for years, but whenever she began a letter she'd become tongue-tied, or whatever the written equivalent was, and unable to carry on. She had never asked him for one red cent to help raise Shelby, and Shelton had never inquired about him. Perhaps he could not let on that his heart was every bit as crushed as Eileen's. At least she liked to think so. Shelton had his position to consider, his reputation as an author. And at least Eileen hadn't starved.

But of all the men she'd known, and loved or not loved, and bedded down, and wedded and unwedded, Shelton was the one she remembered, as if he had planted a little fish-hook in her heart and still had the power to tug on it, even over the distance of all these years.

She leafed to the back of the autograph book and found that Dwight had scrawled in his ugly boy's hand, "By hook or by crook, I'll be last in the book." Crammed down in the corner below that was an even homelier scrawl: "No you won't. Aubrey." She sighed, thinking back to a time when dealing with her brothers' relentless campaign of teasing had been her worst problem. Then had come sex, a brief flood of almost unbelievable bliss, followed by the hard clamp of consequences.

Eileen heard Bernadette in the bathroom going through her elaborate preparations for going out in public—drawing tiny individual black lashes below her startling green eyes, meticulously varnishing her full lips with Yardley's Carnaby Pink Slicker. She couldn't work at the Fry King for much longer, with her belly becoming so obvious. It was good of Salem and Stella to have given her the job for the summer, but as usual, the kindness of the townsfolk was tinged with a certain condescension.

"Mother, can I borrow a few bucks?" Bernadette emerged from the steamy bathroom wearing a yellow terry-towel, her hair wrapped as if in a turban, looking lithe, innocent, and shockingly beautiful. No wonder they get pregnant so easily, her mother thought.

"But you get paid tomorrow, don't you?"

"I'm going to the A & Dub with the kids tonight. I only need enough for a root beer and some Coney fries."

"Honestly, Bernadette, I wish you'd eat properly." Eileen fished out three wrinkled dollar bills from a small tea tin beside the canister of flour. "Give me back the change," she said.

The phone jangled, and she wondered with a small, involuntary thrill if it was Herb. It was as if her body's pilot light had been recently re-lit, so that a surge of arousal could be triggered by the mere ringing of a bell.

"Hello?"

"Eileen." The voice was so shrill she had to hold the receiver away from her ear.

"*Mother?*"

"Don't sound so surprised. Tell me. How many husbands are you going to bring?"

"To the reunion?"

"No, to the public hanging. What did you think?"

"Oh, Mother. I haven't given it much thought. The children are all coming, with their kids, of course. Why do you need to know?"

"We have to feed everyone. Turning ninety is costing me a bloody fortune. Maybe I should die now and save the trouble."

Eileen had mixed feelings about that. "Well, of course Howard will be there."

"You mean Soapy. Nobody calls him Howard."

"And I guess I should ask Robbie, since he still lives in town."

"That fruit? Won't there be talk?"

"No more than there was when you got us married

off." Eileen's voice was hardening into irritation.

"Is that Shelby coming?"

"I hope so."

"Not with a boyfriend?"

"That's entirely up to him. If he wants to bring his roommate, then that's fine."

"Eileen, honestly, couldn't you have nipped it in the bud?"

"Nipped what in the bud?"

"You know what I mean. Don't pretend you don't."

"Shelby's a good man and I'm as proud of him as all the rest of my children. He's every bit as talented and sensitive as his father." Eileen realized as soon as the words were out that it was the wrong thing to say.

"Let's not get started on that. So from your side there'll be—let's see, kids, ex-husbands and their wives, grand-kids—merciful Jesus, that must be close to forty people."

"At least."

"Can't you cut it down to—say, ten?"

"Which one of my children should I leave out?" Eileen was becoming frankly exasperated, with the hope-less, suffocated feeling she always had when Min came into her mind.

"Bernadette won't be interested in all this, will she?" The old buzzard was trying to sound innocent.

Now her blood was up. Irish pipes sounded inaudi-bly in the background, and the pound of drums. "Mother. Get this through your head. *Bernadette is coming to the reunion.*" Eileen wondered if this was the real reason Min had called.

"I was only thinking of her condition," Min backpedalled.

"Goodbye, Mother. Thank you for calling," Eileen said firmly, setting down the receiver. The phone immediately rang again.

"Is Bernadette there?" Heavens, which boy was this? He sounded too old, as if he were in his twenties.

"She just left for work. Who's calling?"

"A friend. Thanks, Mrs. Smith."

"It's Connar now."

"Sorry. Thanks, Mrs. Connar."

She put down the receiver and it rang again.

"Hello."

"Excuse me. That Mrs. Smith?"

"Connar."

"Oh well then, Mrs. Connar. This is the clinic calling. Sophie's going to need surgery on her liver."

"Oh, no. Not—cancer, is it?"

"We're not sure. She'll have to stay here for a few more days for a series of tests."

"Poor dear. Well, go ahead with them then."

"That's the thing, Mrs. Connar. You see, it's going to be sort of . . . expensive, all these tests, and since your bills have been in arrears . . ."

"But if the poor creature's sick . . ." They'd had Sophie since Bernadette was born, a white cloud of Persian fur and uncanny blue eyes.

"I'm afraid you owe us $149, Mrs. Connar. That's before the surgery, which will be another $89."

"For a *cat?*"

"She'll need an anaesthetic, a biopsy, and a lot of other tests beside."

"Is there nothing else we can do?"

"Of course it would be cheaper just to have her . . .

you know, put down. But you'd still owe us the $149, plus the charges for having her put to sleep."

"I'll find the money," Eileen gasped, her heart pounding. "Go ahead with the surgery." She hung up the phone, her face crumpling into tears. Then she heard a tap at the door. *Shave and a haircut, two bits.* "Their" knock. It was Herb. He'd timed his arrival with Bernadette's departure.

Eileen's heart lifted, not so much with the promise of sex as the hope of financial rescue. She knew Herb would ask no questions, and not be in a hurry for her to repay the nearly $250 it would take to save her cat. She went to the door, wiping her eyes and pinching her cheeks to pinkness, thanking God that delivery from trouble could come in such unexpected forms.

13.

A summer evening in Harman was all that anyone could ask for. The air was sweet with humidity and heavy with scent. It smelled like sweet peas, overheated lilacs, phlox nodding on bruised stems. The sexual hiss of cicadas, seductive as a cobra, gave way to the cooler, mintier sound of crickets. The evening melted easily on the tongue, leaving an aftertaste like lilies of the valley.

Dot had a beauty of her own, a great self-possession, and even an air of purpose which was palpable in the way she trod the sidewalks of Hawthorne Avenue, her eyes cast on the ground. Dot was looking for something. It was a finding expedition. For all her seeming strangeness, her outworldness, she had a jeweller's eye for detail. Suddenly, like a bird of prey, she dove. Her hand snatched something out of the shadows, then deposited it in a cracked black vinyl purse slung over her left arm.

What people didn't seem to realize was that there was perfectly good tobacco left in those butts. It tasted a little stale, but when neatly re-rolled into a fresh paper (one of Dot's many skills, like mixing a brilliant Manhattan or knitting tablecloths of fine lace) it was hard to distinguish from the real thing.

Sometimes she found money on the ground, coins

mostly, which she figured were hers as much as anyone else's. The odd time that she found a wallet, she felt badly about taking out the bills and usually decided to leave it lay. But emptying out a change purse was another matter entirely.

This evening was no different from any other except for a preponderance of cigar butts, which she disdained. She liked the smell of fresh cigar smoke on a man, the way it clung to his shirt and flavoured his breath, but she had no desire to take that strong taste directly into her mouth.

There was a slight stirring in the bushes. This Dot noticed. She was always on the lookout for cats, which was something the people of Harman could not understand. Her house, a sagging relic she had inherited from a senile great-uncle, stank of cat pee, and every surface was worn by claws. The furniture was liberally matted with cushions of multicoloured fur. Her cats were family. All were tenderly fed and individually named. She even baptized them out in the backyard under the rusted old pump. This prompted a neighbour to start a rumour: "Dot's drowning her cats."

Dot would never do such a thing. She rescued kittens tied up in sacks in the river. She sewed up the tattered remnants of tomcat ears with needle and thread. She had no money to have them spayed, or "spaded" as people insisted on calling it, so new litters were frequent. The death of a cat grieved her for weeks.

Dot began to feel around in the trembling bushes blindly with one hand, searching for fur. Instead she touched skin. The rustling increased. Dot grabbed, and there was a cry, high and a bit unnatural. She let go, leaning in close to have a look.

A face looked back at her from the deeps of shadow, a small pointed face with enormous brown eyes. It showed no fear, and no hope. It reminded Dot of the way a cat would relax into her hands when it was ready to die.

"What's your name?" After a long pause, she repeated the question.

Then the creature answered.

"What's your name?"

"Dot."

"Dot." Then she realized they were not having a conversation, after all. She parted the bushes and the child shrank back, not in terror, but as a reflex of withdrawal.

"You can come out if you want." Dot began to rummage in her bags for something enticing and came up with a hard orange coconut ball from the penny candy section of Peck's Grocery. It was dusty from the burlap, but candy nonetheless. She turned it between thumb and forefinger like a jewel.

"Candy," she said.

"Candy." The child, whom she could now see was a small, slight boy dressed in a too-large faded shirt and handed-down shorts, climbed out and reached for the sweet. Dot backed up a few steps and he followed her, his hand outstretched. Dot noticed that he walked stiffly on the tips of his toes.

She gave him the coconut ball, which he looked at intently before smelling it, then popping it into his mouth. Dot offered her hand, and he stared at it as if he had never seen a human hand before.

"Would you like to come to my house?"

"My house."

"Yes, my house. You can look at my cats."

"Cats." He seemed to have some idea of what the word meant. He would not take her hand, but followed her like an automaton. Dot wondered how long it had been since the child had eaten.

It was a long walk back to Dot's house, and the whole distance she prayed they would not run into anyone she knew. Or even someone she didn't know. Dot knew enough about what people thought of her to be leery of being seen with a child. In fact, some of the local children were afraid of her, believing she was a bit of a witch. The thought did not displease her, and she did nothing to dispel it.

Someone or something must have been protecting the pair of them that evening, for they saw no one, friend or foe. The small boy walked straight into Dot's slouching old house trustingly—but no, it wasn't that. There was a lack of fear, to be certain. But a lack of anything else as well. He walked in completely neutral, as if this smelly old place were the same as any other.

When the door swung closed, cats stirred from every corner. They raised their heads from torn, mildewed sofas, crawled out from behind tables, jumped down from the mantlepiece. All were hungry and mewed and yowled piteously. "All right, my beauties. Soon, soon. Come meet my visitor."

The cats flocked around Dot, wrapping themselves with sinful sensuality around her bare legs and reaching up to claw at her skirts. They did not go near the child, who stood and stared with eyes as bright and unknowing as a baby bird's. "Come help me feed the beauties," Dot said, and he followed her into the kitchen like a sleepwalker.

Dot would buy cat food before groceries for herself,

and she took down several large cans of Puss N' Boots Deluxe Salmon Treat from a well-stocked cupboard while the cats swarmed darkly around her ankles. A small orange-and-white tabby had begun to climb her leg. Dot opened the cans and emptied them into a dozen cracked plastic bowls, then tenderly sprinkled the fishy mush with dry kibbles of Purina: "Crunchy bits!" she cried, knowing how much they loved them. The boy stared at Dot the whole time, hardly noticing the cats. As she set down the bowls all over the kitchen, she wondered what on earth she was going to give the child to eat.

Dot did not have a refrigerator. Though she did occasionally buy half-and-half for the cats, it never lasted long enough for her to need one. Her own diet was haphazard, whatever came to hand, and like manna in the wilderness, enough always appeared day by day to sustain her. But a child was another matter. He needed wholesome food, the things she remembered from her childhood—boiled puddings, sausages, fried bread with pork gravy. She rummaged in the cupboard and found a dented can with no label on it.

"Shall we take potluck?" The boy did not react, but when she began to open the can he came a little closer, perhaps drawn by the smell. "We're in luck! It's people food. Beefaroni! Do you like Beefaroni?" She held the can under his nose and he plucked out a morsel, shoving it into his mouth.

One burner on her gas stove still worked, and she managed to find a pot with no handle on it and an old black spoon. She sat the boy down on a kitchen chair and he remained perched there, doll-like, while she prepared the simple meal.

While she cooked, she thought. Somehow the boy must have become separated from his parents. Or was it something worse than that? Dot well knew the penalties of not being normal. Abandonment was almost to be expected.

As she lifted the steaming pot off the stove, the boy absolutely astounded her by speaking spontaneously.

"Mum," he said.

Dot wasn't at all sure how to take this. Was he already seeing her as a mother figure (too much to hope for, she felt), or crying out for his own mother?

"Where's your Mum?" Dot tried to look into his evasive eyes.

"Mum." He said it without emotion, as if stating a fact.

"Yes, but . . ." How was she going to get through to him? "I'm Dot. Where's your Mum?"

There was no response. Dot found a bowl that didn't have cat food in it and emptied most of the steaming Beefaroni into it. The child began to attack it with his hands.

"Careful, you'll burn yourself. I'm afraid all we have to drink is water. Here's a spoon." She wondered if he knew how to use one, but he took it in his left hand and began to feed himself, getting most of it in his mouth. Dot sat down at the table with him, finishing the rest of the bland, viscous meal out of the pot with the serving spoon. She blew on each mouthful before eating it, and before long the boy began to imitate her, not in play but very solemnly. It was as close to a game as they were going to get, Dot realized. So she blew elaborately, theatrically, with an exaggerated facial expression, and the child responded by blowing on the spoon so hard the food flew across the room. Dot laughed and the boy looked startled.

"I have to call you something. How about Gareth?"

"Gareth." She took that as a sign that he approved. The name was just odd enough to suit him, she thought. A real name, a name with substance, but not one you heard every day.

Dot was relieved to find he knew how to use the bathroom. It amused her to see him aiming carefully into the bowl; someone had trained him well. The next problem was finding him a bed. All surfaces were cat-claimed, even Dot's own bed, which wasn't really big enough for two. Then she thought of something. She'd dragged a mattress home months ago—someone had put it out with the garbage, a perfectly good matttress, stained and sagging but still in one piece. She found it in the living room, propped against the wall with old clothes draped over it, and wrestled it into her bedroom. Blankets were no problem, though most of them smelled bad and were looped with claw marks. Gareth didn't seem to mind. He let Dot change him into an old men's T-shirt and lay down willingly, obviously exhausted. Dot was about to turn out the light when she thought of something.

She knelt beside Gareth's bed. The boy obviously couldn't manage this, so it was only right that Dot do it for him.

"Now I lay me down to sleep. I pray the Lord my soul to keep. If I should die before I wake . . ." No, that was a horrible prayer. Dot racked her brains. "Lord, make me an instrument of Thy peace." No, too fancy for a kid. Then she decided to improvise.

"Dear Lord, it's me again, Dot. Thank you for bringing

Gareth here to share my roof. Look after both of us, will you, God. Especially watch over Gareth here and keep him out of trouble. I think he's had enough of it already. Well, that's about it for today. In the name of our Lord Jesus Christ, I pray. Amen."

Gareth had already fallen asleep. Dot licked her finger and made the sign of the cross on his forehead. She had gone looking for cigarette butts tonight and had found something else. That's the way life is, she thought. Full of strange blessings. She rolled into bed, and half a dozen cats leaped up to snuggle against her bulky body for the night.

14.

Min Connar peered out through the yellowy lace curtains of her front room to the street outside. It was part of her daily routine. She had to keep track; it was important. Harman might get out of hand without her eternal vigilance. So she needed to watch everyone's comings and goings, to deduce everything that was going on in the town.

Well, for the love of God, would you look at that. A pack of those—*what d'ye call them, anyway? Hippies?*—went strolling past, laughing in a way that suggested drunkenness, or worse. Things were going downhill, there was no doubt about that, and in a hurry, too. Just look at those boys. They had hair almost down to their shoulders, and strange-looking cotton shirts that looked like they'd been hit with an explosion of paint.

In one of her infrequent public appearances, Alma Hudson walked by, probably on the way to Peck's to buy more candy and chips. As if she needed them. Again Min felt she had the inalienable right to be appalled. Such a size. It was even hard for her to walk. Early in the morning and already she was out of breath. A sin to eat that much. Min had always watched her diet, kept her figure. Alma glanced over to the conspicuous gap in the Connars's front curtain and gave a little wave. *Just Min, spying again.*

Disapproving of my size, I suppose. Let her have her pleasure; it's the only one she's got. Min waved back, turning her scowl of disapproval into a false social smile that made her cheek muscles crack.

Then—glory of glories. Who was this? The one she had been hearing about? With his homespun-looking, unbleached cotton shirt without a collar and faded jeans, his leather sandals, the hair and beard and sweet countenance, it could only be the much-talked-about stranger in town, the celebrated Bob. He'd been doing odd jobs, home repairs and the like, and Min had even been tempted to have him in to fix the rotting roof, but Aubrey had protested. ("We don't need Jesus in the house." "Nonsense. He wouldn't even be in the house. He'd be on it." "He'd probably charge too much. I can do it myself." "But you won't. And how do you know he'd charge too much?" "He's probably just a hippie anyway." "No, I hear he's quite smart and doesn't take any drugs." "Then why doesn't he cut his hair?")

Where was Bob headed? Min speculated. Maybe off to do another home repair somewhere. He'd had no problem getting work—it was something about his manner, his politeness. Or was it something else? Min let the curtain drop, shuffling off to find Aubrey so she could badger him some more.

But Bob was off to do a repair of a completely different sort. When Ethel McConnaughey had asked him over for tea the other day, he couldn't imagine what she might want of him. Her house was like stepping backwards in time by thirty years; stuffed with delicate knick-knacks and antique windup toys, ostriches pulling carts and drumming monkeys, with clay sculptures of the weathered faces of sea captains mounted on the wall.

"It's Evan," she'd told him, her voice tight with anxiety. "He hasn't been able to walk for a couple of years now. And he isn't that old. The doctors are of no use to him at all. I couldn't help but hear about Agnes and her kitten. If you don't mind my saying so, it looks to me as if you have something special about you. A gift. Would you mind terribly just talking to Evan some time? Could you say a special prayer for him or something?"

Bob thought about it for a moment. "Mrs. McConnaughey, I'd like nothing better than to help your husband. But sometimes people have to learn to help themselves."

"Exactly! So maybe you could talk some sense into his head. Get him to eat better, maybe, or at least try to move around more. He's let this thing beat him, you know."

"Not necessarily."

"Could you do it for me? I'd be so very grateful." Ethel was close to tears now, and Bob reached over and put his hand on her wrist.

"I'll see him. I can't guarantee anything, of course. But I'll talk to him. Try to give him some hope. I'll bring some reading material. Might inspire him."

"I don't know how to thank you."

"But I haven't done anything yet." Bob showed his even white teeth in a pleasant smile that slightly increased Ethel's pulse.

"I have every faith in you," she answered. And she insisted he take a fresh rhubarb pie with him back to the small basement apartment he was renting from the Danvilles.

Now he headed back to the McConnaughey house with a certain sense of purpose. He had gathered enough information from his chat with Ethel, and a brief talk with poor rigid Evan, to feel sure of his course of action. By the time he got to the front door Ethel was beaming in anticipation.

"Bob! So good to see you again."

"That was a delicious pie, Mrs. McConnaughey."

"Please. Ethel."

"Ethel. How is Evan feeling today?"

"A little anxious." They stepped into the parlour, and Bob once again had the feeling of being rocketed backwards in time to 1938. "He doesn't know quite what to expect."

"Well, there's really nothing to worry about. I've done some informal studies on nutrition and might be able to help him with supplementation. Whole grains are a big help."

"Will you need anything before you . . . you know . . . go in and talk to him?"

Bob thought for a moment. "I can think of something."

"Just name it."

"A pitcher of lukewarm water."

Ethel was a bit startled. She had visions of Bob taking Evan into the bathroom for a strange ritual, maybe an enema or an impromptu baptism.

"I'll get you some right away." Bob took the pitcher into the bedroom, where Evan sat propped up stiffly in his wheelchair, looking far too old and drawn for a man in his sixties. Bob glanced at Ethel as he closed the door, a look of reassurance. Unable to stand the suspense of waiting, Ethel took her purse and left the house to run a few errands.

Along the way she ran into Aubrey, still in his chipper mood.

"Bob's seeing Evan this morning," she confided in a tone of barely suppressed excitement.

"Oh, you mean Jesus."

"Honestly, Aubrey, you should give him a chance. Such a polite young man."

"Well, Min wants me to get him to fix the roof. So he does miracles on the side, does he?"

"Of course not. But he knows a lot about nutrition. He just might be able to help poor Evan."

"Don't get your hopes too high, Ethel. All sorts of quacks around these days, you know."

"Bob is not a quack."

"But the truth is you don't know anything about him. He might be out to take you for a ride."

"Bob has never once asked for payment. He does this out of the goodness of his heart."

"Well, I hope so, for your sake, Ethel. Give my best to Evan." He tipped an imaginary hat (hats having fallen out of fashion quite suddenly in the last couple of years) and sauntered on, wondering if he should give this Bob a call. He might be good for Min, fresh prey for the old spider, and something to get her mind off that bloody reunion. The phone calls to Portadown alone were costing a fortune, and Connar and Pedlow relatives were beginning to ooze out of the woodwork like slime. "Speak up!" Min would shout over the long-distance wires. "I can't understand your accent. Your *accent!* No, you're the one talking strangely. Don't be impertinent with me, young man!" It was enough to give Aubrey a headache.

Two hours had gone by since Ethel had left Bob alone with Evan, and now she approached the house with a strange mixture of light-hearted anticipation and sick dread. This was almost like the night of her wedding, when she'd had no idea of what was going to happen to her next. Surely Evan could be no worse off than he was before, could he?

She came in the front entrance, then heard loud voices behind the bedroom door, followed by a burst of laughter. It was almost as if they were celebrating something. The door suddenly popped open, and Ethel sat down hard on the living room sofa.

For there was Bob, standing with his arm around an upright Evan, who began to walk forward in slow, shuffling steps, his usually grey face pinkening with delight. "Ethie!" he cried, and Ethel had to take a deep breath because she felt a little woozy. "Ethie, I'm walking!"

"How on earth—Bob, it's a miracle!"

"Evan was very cooperative," Bob said modestly, helping him take a slow but purposeful tour of the hallway.

"But I don't understand what happened. Bob, what did you do?"

"We had a talk." Bob looked at Evan with a grin. "We spoke of many things."

"Yes, many things," said Evan.

"I gave him a couple of things to read. A book by Adelle Davis. And one by Kahlil Gibran. Just some good basic reading material."

Ethel looked skeptical. "Come now. There had to be more to it than that. Tell me what else you did."

"Freshie," said Evan.

"What?"

"Freshie. He made me some lukewarm raspberry Freshie with no sugar in it. My God, it was awful. Made me drink six glasses of the stuff."

"It's the Vitamin C," Bob said, guiding Evan into a living room chair. "With a long-term deficiency, it can sometimes have dramatic results, particularly in liquid form."

"Bob says I'm to eat three oranges a day."

"Sakes," said Ethel. No one ate that much fruit.

"And only whole grain bread. And lots of vegetables, leafy green vegetables."

"Evan, I've been trying to get you to eat vegetables for our entire marriage." She thought of the canned peas, the long-boiled spinach, the pale mushy parsnips like carrots that had had a fright.

"Evan's a changed man, Ethel. He'll be taking a good long walk outside every day, rain or shine, and doing some yoga stretching exercises I've given him to keep limbered up. And another thing."

"A dog," said Evan.

"A what?"

"We're getting a dog." He was beaming, pleased as a small boy.

"I really think a pet would help Evan, Ethel. It'd give him a reason to go out and walk. And something to take care of."

"But aren't I enough?"

"Aw, Ethie. You're so independent, you can take care of yourself." His voice faltered. "It was getting so's I thought you didn't need me, with me being so useless and all."

"Evan."

"It's true. Ever since I retired . . ."

"But all that's going to change now, Evan," Bob piped up. "This is the start of a new life. A healthy life. I know you'll want to help Evan every step of the way, Ethel."

"I'm sure." Ethel wasn't sure at all. She felt upstaged,

as if her vegetables suddenly weren't good enough. And a dog would make such a mess, the hair and fleas.

"It takes some getting used to," Bob said compassionately, noticing her confusion and doubt. "It's an adjustment. But both of you will be healthier in the long run. You might be able to take little trips together. You told me you'd always wanted to travel, Ethel."

"Did you?" asked Evan.

It was all too much to take in. Ethel insisted Bob stay for supper, and he helped her cook, advising her on the proper way to lightly steam the cabbage, not boiling it grey the way Mother had taught her. They admitted it did taste better that way, more flavourful. Bob told her she could buy an earthenware pot and slow-roast the corned beef in a low oven for eight hours, letting it cook in its own juices. It was whole new way of thinking. Ethel's head was in a whirl.

But Evan was walking. "How shall I ever repay you for this?" she asked him as he stood in the doorway to say good night. Evan stood beside her, his only support a gold-headed cane.

"I don't need to be repaid."

"But surely—"

"Ethel, maybe it's better if you don't tell too many people about this. They might get the wrong idea. Just say that Evan's following a new diet."

"Whatever you wish, Bob. Thank you so much— you're a godsend."

When she closed the door, she remembered the gospel lesson about the little girl being raised from the dead, and the hair on her arms stood up as stiffly as if she'd just received a terrible shock.

15.

The Reverend Ninian Sanderson was in fine form that Sunday morning at St. Andrew's United Church. Most of his sermons went along smoothly enough, with lots of scriptural references to make them relevant, but they usually lacked a central idea. Without something to unify his thoughts, the good Reverend had a tendency to ramble and digress. Passion was out of the question—this was the United Church, after all, not some collection of babbling fools like those people down the street at Pentecostal Holiness. But this morning was the exception. Nin Sanderson was downright exercised, moved by disapproval into an unusual fit of eloquence.

"Beware of false prophets," he intoned in a voice that made the elderly women in the back row pop their half-closed eyes open, "which come to you in sheep's clothing, but inwardly they are ravening wolves. In this I quote the Book of Matthew, Chapter 7, Verse 15. And the following: 'For false Christs and false prophets shall rise, and shall show signs and wonders, to seduce, if it were possible, even the elect.' St. Mark, 13:22."

A few congregational members began to riffle discreetly through the thin rice-paper pages of their Bibles to find these quotes.

"I tell you, these words are as relevant today as when they were penned by the saints of old. *False prophets.* They're everywhere, my friends. On your television screens, pitching you the good life in those wretched commercials for Winston cigarettes and Molson's beer."

Aubrey Connar sat in a front-row pew with Min, wondering if God really had it in for specific name brands like that, or if Nin were merely using them as an example. Was it less godly to smoke Winstons than Salems? Were some brands, like Export A for example, officially sanctioned by the church? It gave a whole new meaning to the expression "holy smokes."

"But they're not just on your TV screen any more. They lurk among us, corrupting our young people with shallow promises of 'peace' and 'love.' These self-appointed Messiahs, many of whom are not even of the Christian faith, have woven a spell around the youth of today, promising spiritual enlightenment through such questionable practices as chanting and meditation."

A verse from one of the Psalms popped into Aubrey's head: "I remember the days of old, I meditate on all thy works; I muse on the work of thy hands." But the Psalms were just a bunch of old Hebrew nonsense, weren't they?

Nin, so worked up that he felt a bit choked, paused for a drink of water, noticing how attentive his audience looked. Even shocked. They weren't used to the Reverend raising his voice. But some of them were thinking, "It's about time somebody spoke out against those god-damned hippies."

Aubrey was amused. This was the first time he'd seen old Nin so wrought up about anything. He'd brought Min along to church this morning—a major operation requiring all the planning and preparation of a military exercise—and noticed with hidden pleasure her scowl of disapproval at Nin's fit of pique. It just wasn't proper for ministers to be angry about anything. They were, after all, men of God, modelling themselves on gentle Jesus meek and mild.

"Has anyone here heard of a certain personage called His Holiness the Maharishi Mahesh Yogi? Does that name startle you? It should. This foreign-born, self-appointed prophet is the leading proponent of something he calls 'Transcendental Meditation.' I'll repeat that: *Tran-scen-dental Med-i-ta-tion.* This dubious exercise involves sitting down on the floor all twisted up into a pretzel, closing your eyes, and saying, '*Ohmmmmm . . .*'"

There were titters from the crowd. Good, good. Ninian Sanderson wanted the whole of Harman—well, the churchgoing folk of Harman, who were the only souls worth bothering with—to realize just how ridiculous this whole thing was.

"The Maharishi is not telling the young people of the world to read their Bibles. The Maharishi is not telling them to attend church on Sundays or respect their elders. He's telling them to squinch up their eyeballs and say, '*Ohmmmmm . . .*'"

This time there was out-and-out laughter, the first time Aubrey could ever remember such a phenomenon in church. Min looked confused and not very pleased. This was leading somewhere; she knew it.

"But we don't have to look to the Maharishi Mahesh Yogi to find examples of people being led astray by false prophets who aren't even of the Christian faith. It happens right here in our very own community of Harman."

There was an absolute, utter silence in the church. The congregation was rapt, held in suspension. It was both awful and beautiful, Aubrey thought. Worth the price of admission, for once.

"Some of you may have heard that certain people in Harman have been led astray by an interloper, a young man who shall remain nameless."

"He means Bob," Min sputtered to Aubrey, who shushed her.

"This young man, who apparently has no Christian background whatsoever, purports to heal people by the laying on of hands. There is not one shred of evidence that this young man has any healing ability whatsoever, yet he has the effrontery to claim that, like Our Lord Himself, he can relieve people of their ailments."

Everyone in the congregation was thinking the same thing: that just this past week they'd seen Evan McConnaughey out and about on one of his little walks, with Ethel hanging on his arm, barely able to keep up with him. Both of them were beaming in an expression half wonderstruck, half frightened. There was even talk that they were looking around for a suitable dog.

"Beware the false prophets, who arrogantly assume the awesome power of God. They shall fall, like the prophets of antiquity. 'I am the Lord thy God, which brought thee out of the land of Egypt, from the house of bondage. *Thou shalt have none other gods before me.*' Beware of wolves in sheep's clothing! Resist their spell, their wayward promises, and cleave to the faith of our fathers!"

This would be a perfect place for a hymn, Aubrey thought: "And now, a word from our sponsors." But no, Nin wasn't finished yet.

"Rigourously question the motives of anyone claiming to have holy powers, for you may be in the grip of a charlatan." Some people were nodding vigorously. Others looked disappointed. They had so wanted to believe in Bob. A distant, too-exalted Christ was so hard to hold on to. What a wonder to walk beside him, even in imagination! And didn't Jesus himself say that we had to be prepared every hour, every day, in case the moment of his second coming was truly at hand?

At that precise instant, the back entrance of the church popped open, and God walked in the door.

All heads turned. No one ever came late. It simply wasn't done. Not only that, but God had a big fat unabashed smile on his face, radiating positive energy at the congregation, many of whom couldn't resist smiling back.

It was just that he looked so friendly. Even Reverend Sanderson caught the warm beam of his smile sweeping like the brilliant illuminating flash of a lighthouse in his direction. Bob sat down in an empty rear pew, looking genuinely pleased to be there. All at once Nin's rhetoric turned to stone in his throat.

"Please turn to number 147 in your hymnary," he choked, completely caught off guard by the unexpected guest appearance of the One in his church. "Fairest Lord Jesus."

The congregation stood while Bertha MacAdam pumped the wheezy old pipe organ with her feet and began to sing the lovely old hymn with its unbearably beautiful words:

"Fair are the meadows, fairer still the woodlands,
Robed in the blooming garb of spring;

Jesus is fairer, Jesus is purer,

Who makes the troubled heart to sing."

And a strange thing began to happen to the congregation of St. Andrew's United Church that morning, a thing that had never happened to them before. They began to weep. Not just the women. Grown men who never showed emotion felt choked by the beauty of that hymn. Min pulled a yellowy lace-bordered handkerchief out of her sleeve and covered her mouth, which had stretched open in an involuntary sob. Even Aubrey turned away and pretended to cough.

It was just that they had never before felt the astounding sensation of the fairest of all creation standing among them. Their yearned-for Saviour was no longer some remote figurehead or sanitized cartoon figure from a Sunday school paper. There was the most uncanny feeling in the air in that moment that Jesus, so much fairer and purer than anything they could even imagine, was actually *here*.

Nin realized too late that he'd picked the wrong hymn and that the congregation was being affected by some kind of mass mesmerism. This was exactly the sort of thing he'd been trying to preach against, but as he stood at the front facing the wet-eyed, swaying crowd, he too began to feel unaccountably moved. It was the strangest thing, and it scared him. Church was not the place for showing emotions. Well, perhaps at a wedding or a funeral, but even there you had to be careful not to get too carried away. There was a right and a wrong way to grieve or rejoice. But how to account for these tears, this awe? Something very powerful was overflowing the container here, and Ninian saw it as a serious threat to his ministry.

He was relieved when everyone sat down after the final amen, and when all the nose-blowing and throat-clearing had finally ended he launched into the weekly announcements.

"The church maintenance committee is currently looking for volunteers to do some serious repairs to the building." At this he looked a little weary, as no one ever seemed to want to help out here. "Among other things, the roof badly needs fixing as it leaks every time it rains. Are any among you willing to give some of your time and effort to this worthy cause?"

"I will!" piped up a voice from the back row.

"Sweet Jesus," said Aubrey under his breath. Everyone knew that Nin's question had been a rhetorical one. No one was ever expected to actually pop up and volunteer. Perhaps that was why there was never anyone around to fix the roof.

Bob stood up without a trace of self-consciousness and looked directly at Nin, who took a small involuntary step backwards. "I'd be happy to help with repairs. I even have my own set of tools, thanks to the generosity of someone I worked for in town. Just tell me what needs to be done."

"Thank you, young man." Ninian looked flushed and uneasy. No one knew where to look.

"Bob," he said, beaming, and sat down again. Confusion swept over the crowd. Nin felt he was losing control of things again and launched into his final prayer, fortunately pre-written so all he had to do was read from the script. At this the people settled down a little bit, falling into their customary light doze. Then came the benediction, and the choir stood up and sang the threefold amen.

As he strode down the aisle to stand at the back of the church and shake people's hands, Nin prayed the young man would leave quickly. But no, he stayed, and he mingled. He seemed to know an incredible number of people in the congregation, and they reacted to him very warmly.

"Aubrey! Go on over and ask him to fix our roof. Clean out the gutters, too, while he's at it."

"He's busy, Min." A great number of people were pressing towards Bob, he noticed, and they seemed to want to touch him, to clasp his hand for a moment, or just to stand in his presence.

Bob made his way down the line to shake hands with Reverend Sanderson. When it was his turn, he introduced himself with impeccable manners, then said, "I loved that last hymn. I'm a baptized Lutheran and I remember singing that one as a little boy."

"Did you, now."

"Do you need tenors in the choir?"

Ninian was completely flabbergasted. His eyes were bulging a bit. "You'll have to ask Bertha."

"Well, let me know when you need me to do the repairs. Here, take one of these." Nin stood there astonished as Bob pulled out a small white card, hand-lettered with his address and phone number in fine calligraphy.

"God has business cards," Aubrey murmured, witnessing the incredible scene.

"What're you talking about? You're letting him get away!" Min trundled up to Bob and gripped his wrist in her gnarled bluish hand. "I'll have one of those cards, too, dear," she said, forcing sweetness into her cracked crone's voice.

"Surely, ma'am." Bob favoured her with one of those cloudlike, heavenly smiles.

"I'll be calling on you soon." She smiled back at him, showing her ancient dentures, and Aubrey felt a little sick. The lad was entertaining enough, especially the way he was taking in everybody in town, but Aubrey didn't want to have to deal with him directly.

Something about him made him a little uncomfortable. He couldn't put his finger on it, and he didn't want to. In his mind, he pulled the shade down tight. *Leave it alone*, he thought. We've enough to worry about in this family already.

Then a worried-looking young woman took Bob aside; Aubrey heard her say something about her daughter's terrible sore throats. He hoped Ninian didn't overhear the conversation. You couldn't bar Jesus from a church, now, could you? Aubrey found the whole thing amusing. The interloper had crashed the gates, and there hadn't been a thing Nin could do about it. Would Bob be a regular feature at church from now on? It might almost be worth it to attend more often, even though Min would probably insist on coming with him. Perhaps it was good for her; she hadn't staged a death in some time now. Call it a resurrection. Apparently Bob was already having his effects.

16.

Mrs. Wilhelmina Peck knew that something was up. It had to do with that Dot. Hadn't Mrs. Peck been saying for years now that something needed to be done about Dot? For the love of Harry, a person couldn't go on that way, just . . . But there you were, no one listened. And now something really peculiar was starting to happen.

Dot was buying things. Specifically, she was buying things at Peck's, like cereal. Dot had never eaten cereal in all her life as far as anyone in Harman knew (and believe me, they knew). She was buying kiddie-type cereal too, kinds like Post Krispy Kritters and Kellogg's Puffa Puffa Rice. Had she gone off her head completely?

There she was right now, buying a quart bottle of homo milk. If she wanted milk, which she never did before, why didn't she get it delivered like everyone else did? Dot just had to be contrary; that's all there was to it.

But this time it was different. Dot had seldom bought anything much at Peck's before, except the odd block of Ingersoll cheese (Dot loved cheese). Now she was buying things like milk and cereal and peanut butter and potatoes and bread and bologna, and once, even a small steak.

Did she have a man? Wilhelmina wondered as Dot pushed a rickety old cart around the store, plucking this and that off the shelves and flinging it in. As far as anyone knew (and believe me, they didn't), Dot had never had a boyfriend and in fact had no interest in men at all. This revealed the myopic perception of the good folk of Harman, as in her day Dot had been quite a looker, not beautiful but striking, mysterious almost, a Mata Hari type. You could still see it in the eyes. In her twenties she had borne an uncanny resemblance to Theda Bara, a silent-screen heroine whose name was an anagram for Arab Death.

But that was then, before Dot had gone off her rocker and inherited that disgrace of a house from her loony great-uncle Morton. Of course it was well known that Dot had money salted away, likely crammed into a mouldy old mattress somewhere. "She'll probably leave it all to her cats," folks said, little realizing that Dot had already given away a large chunk of her inheritance to the United Negro College Fund, a charity she had seen advertised on TV. That was Dot's way—throwing her money away like it was nothing, and never mind the consequences.

Now she began to unload her cart at the checkout, as usual not saying a word. "Lovely day," Mrs. Peck remarked. Dot nodded. "My goodness, Dot. This is a lot of food for one person. Are you having a party?"

"That's it," said Dot. It sounded like a good enough explanation to her.

"Who's coming?"

"Everybody who's anybody. Mostly the Fenians."

Trust Dot to say something crazy. "Well, I hope you have a good time. That will be $8.79."

Dot shook her head. It had been a while since she had bought food, and the prices now were positively scandalous. Especially the Beefaroni.

The bell dinged as Dot swept out of the store with her brown paper bags. At that instant Agnes Flood, who'd been lurking discreetly in the produce section, scuttled over to Mrs. Peck with a head of lettuce. "Did you ever see the like!" she exclaimed, clearly excited by this new development.

"Yes, and I've heard she's buying other odd things as well."

"Clothing." Agnes was clearly up on the story. "Someone saw her in the Metropolitan store looking in the *children's wear* department."

"Yes, I heard she bought—*underwear.*" The two gazed at each other in rapt fascination.

"And she's been going in to Ann Frickert's shop, too." Nobody in Harman would admit to going in there, as it was a second-hand store full of old junk and even older clothes, smelly, saggy, and sad.

"Where does she get the money, I wonder? Everyone gives her handouts, but lately she's been living it up."

"Oh well, you know, her uncle . . ."

"That's old news. They say all that money is gone now. Frittered away. I hear she used to gamble."

"I wouldn't be too sure about that," Agnes said. Her teeth were firmly into this subject and she wasn't about to loosen her grip.

Mrs. Peck savored a good nibble, too. "You mean you believe all those stories about the stock market?"

"Dot's smarter than she looks."

"You don't suppose she's starting to dress up her cats. Remember that artist, what's her name anyways, with the monkey in the baby carriage?"

"I hope not. Does she have dolls?"

"No, but there's a scarecrow in her backyard. She calls it Pierre Elliot Trudeau. I asked her why and she said, 'It looks like he's shrugging.'"

"She says such queer things."

"Queer is no word for it."

"Well, Willie, I'll have to get going now. Shelton will want his lunch. Bacon, lettuce, and tomato sandwiches."

"And how is Bob?" Wilhelmina's face visibly softened when she spoke his name.

"Oh, we really miss him since he got his own place. But he's doing so well right now. He's started his own little business. He's a carpenter, you know."

"Is he, now."

"Well, more of a jack-of-all-trades. So handy. He can fix anything—broken toilets, squeaky doors—even TVs. He's putting half the tradesmen of Harman out of business. But everybody likes him. And he'll give you nutrition advice on the side, for free."

"Have you seen—"

"Evan? Well, everyone thinks it's such a miracle," she beamed, "but I knew it would happen because of Muffin. Muffin was the first."

"Evan's got himself a pug."

"I've seen it. Its little nose looks just like wrinkled black velvet."

"Ethel isn't too sure about it. Says he piddled on the rug the first day they had him, but he was probably just nervous."

"I think it's sweet to see them out walking. And it's all Bob's doing. Bob is so special."

"Tell that to Nin Sanderson." The two of them burst out laughing. Bob had been so helpful and had donated so much time to St. Andrews, it was driving Nin crazy. Next he'd be asking to teach Sunday school. Bob was a baptized Christian, which was something, but what sort of strange ideas might he put in the little ones' heads?

"Teach 'em how to walk on water," Aubrey grumbled. He was still balking at calling the number on the small white card Min had shoved in his face. In fact he hadn't even looked at it.

As the Bob story burbled away on the back burners of Harman like a rich and sustaining stew, Dot made her way home with her bags of provisions. Looking after a child was such a responsibility. Fortunately Gareth had no interest at all in playing outside. He just sort of sat and twiddled. Reading him stories did no good, as he couldn't seem to follow the thread of them. Besides, the Grimms's fairy tales Dot read to him out of the only children's book in the house were gruesome, full of maiming, imprisonment, and death. Not exactly the ideal way to prepare small children for dealing with the world.

Dot did have a TV, an enormous old Marconi with a tiny screen that flipped more often than not. Something wrong with the horizontal hold. In the mornings she would put on Jack LaLanne's exercise show and the trim, jumpsuited figure would leap about with organ music playing in the background. Gareth would stare at the screen, and he seemed to pay especial attention when a large white dog came on the screen.

One day Jack decided to demonstrate just how atrocious the typical North American diet was. He threw raw eggs and uncooked bacon and doughnuts and cups of coffee and hamburgers and french fries and chocolate cake into a big pot and stirred it all around. "Cigarettes! Let's not forget cigarettes!" he cried, crumbling a few into the mixture. Then he presented it to his dog, who for a second appeared quite eager to dig in. Then Jack jerked the mixture away from him. "See, even a dog won't eat it!" he exclaimed.

Dot wondered if Gareth really knew what was going on. *"Inhale!"* Jack would bellow, and the organ played a glissando up the scale. *"Exhale!"* Likewise, a glissando down. Then at the end he always sang, to the tune of the Elvis hit "It's Now or Never":

"It's time to leave you, let's say goodbye.

Each precious moment just seems to fly.

So here's my wish for you—

May the good Lord bless and keep you, too."

Dot never did the exercises, but she always found Jack's sinewy, strenuous goodwill uplifting. It did her good, like the *Mass for Shut-ins* she always watched on Sunday mornings. It mattered not one jot to her that the service was Catholic. Dot was ecumenical in her faith. Nin Sanderson would have referred to her eclectic beliefs as "a dog's breakfast," but never mind; holiness was holiness, wherever you found it.

And Gareth did have a certain something, a quality. His still jet eyes could be compelling when he stared into the middle distance. He was a complete innocent who knew nothing of the brutality of the world. Or at least Dot hoped that he knew nothing. She knew very well, veteran of life that she was, that sooner or later the police would go looking for the child and Dot would have to surrender him. She hoped she didn't go to jail for keeping him this long without reporting it. But she figured it was worth it; prison was a snug, dry place, anyway, preferable to the cardboard box she'd lived in for one whole summer before fortune had given her this house. She'd had it worse, and the pokey offered you three square meals a day plus occupational therapy.

Dot called for him as she opened the front door, hoping the child had been all right on his own for the scant half-hour she'd been away. She found him exactly as he was when she'd left the house, sitting on the sofa with a few of the cats in front of the TV, but not watching it. The program was a cartoon called *The Adventures of Clutch Cargo and his Pals, Spinner and Paddlefoot*. To call it animation was stretching a point. All of Clutch's lines were spoken by the image of a real human mouth superimposed over a wooden-looking still drawing of a face. When the figures walked, their rigid bodies were dragged across the screen. The cartoon reminded Dot a bit of Gareth—surreal, not quite of this world. But Gareth was absorbed in another activity, the same thing he had been doing when Dot left, twirling a button on the sofa cushion around and around and around.

"I've brought you some lunch, Gareth." In spite of his unresponsiveness Dot always spoke to him, with a hunch that he understood more than he let on. "Would you like some Beefaroni?"

That got no response.

"Alpha-Ghetti?"

Suddenly the sofa cushion button popped off in Gareth's hand. "*Ow.*"

"All right. We'll make you some Alpha-Ghetti." Gareth was staring at the button in his hand. Then he pitched it across the room. At least six of the cats pounced on it and Dot laughed. Gareth looked up, startled. She had never seen him laugh or smile. How she longed for it. Those small, pinched features would be completely transformed by a smile.

Maybe he can't think of anything to smile about, Dot mused. It was a feeling she knew only too well.

17.

Bob Hemphill sat in the living room of Ethel and Evan McConnaughey's house in an old-fashioned, bedoileyed rocking chair, a small stack of worn-looking, jacketless books on the floor beside him. A mantle clock ticked loudly, liquidly in the background; if it weren't such a cliché, one might almost be tempted to say that it ticked hypnotically. Bob was surrounded by a small group of women sitting in dining room chairs in a semicircle around him, all leaning ever-so-slightly forward, their eyes slightly glistening with something that went beyond anticipation.

Bob opened one of the books, seemingly at random, and began to read in a delicious baritone voice that would raise the neck hairs of a nun:

"And a woman spoke, saying, 'Tell us of Pain.' And he said: 'Your pain is the breaking of the shell that encloses your understanding. Even as the stone of the fruit must break, that its heart may stand in the sun, so you must know pain.'"

Several of the women were already brimming with tears, though it was hard for them to understand exactly why. In all their lives, they had never heard anything quite as wonderful as this.

"'And could you keep your heart in wonder at the daily miracles of your life, your pain would not seem less wondrous than your joy; and you would accept the seasons of your heart, even as you have always accepted the seasons that pass over your fields. And you would watch with serenity through the winters of your grief.'"

Agnes Flood was now openly weeping. "The seasons of your heart," she murmured to herself. "The winters of your grief." She wanted to remember every word of what he said, so she could write it all down later.

Now Bob dropped the book into his lap and spoke directly to the women, as if he knew it by heart:

"'Much of your pain is self-chosen. It is the bitter potion by which the physician within you heals your sick self. Therefore trust the physician, and drink his remedy in silence and tranquility: For his hand, though heavy and hard, is guided by the tender hand of the Unseen. And the cup he brings, though it burn your lips, has been fashioned of the clay which the Potter has moistened with His own sacred tears.'"

Even Annette Jamieson, mother of that wretched Randy and drippy, whining Denise, seemed to be in a state of rapture, transported. Willie Peck wondered if her blood pressure had gone up, and Pearl Smith badly needed a cigarette. She hadn't told Aubrey she was attending this first meeting of a new society which Ethel was already calling the Church of Bob and wondered what he'd think of all this business.

"That was . . . lovely, Bob," Ethel choked, almost undone by the performance. "Now please excuse me, ladies. And Bob. I must put on the tea." She practically fled the room while Rajah, the new pug, trotted after her, hoping for a Milk Bone or, even better, a red-jelly-centred Peak Frean.

"I am only the messenger," Bob said earnestly, not unaware of the effect he was having on these women. "Look to your own hearts for healing. Let your pain guide you to a new understanding of your own soul." The pug waddled back into the room with a cookie in his mouth and sank down on the floor beside Bob with an asthmatic little wheeze of pleasure.

"Bob . . ." Agnes spoke suddenly, sharply. He knew by her expression that it was costing her something to speak up like this. He gazed at her encouragingly with his tender blue eyes. "I have these . . . things, these heart palpitations. The doctor keeps saying it's nothing, you're too young to worry about it, but how can I get my sleep when I keep waking up with all this banging in my chest? It's terrible—like a conga drum, but not steady at all. Ta-thump, ta-thump . . . then an awful sort of pause, as if my heart has forgotten how to beat . . . then, *whump*, one hard bang, and a flood of these awful palpitations, like I'm rolling down the side of a hill and can't put on the brakes. The doctor says it's only nerves and I should try taking some Librium, but I don't want to take pills. What can I do?"

Bob sat in deep silence for a moment, then astounded the women in the small circle when he got up out of his chair, reached over, and pressed his right hand firmly on Agnes's upper chest. She pinkened all over in a mottled sort of pattern, like diaper rash, as Bob closed his eyes and read the secrets of her heart.

A certain tension ran like piano wire through the room. It was as if there was a silent tug-of-war going on:

loyalty to Bob on one end, and on the other, the ladies'
deep-rooted sense of propriety. Why, Bob was practically
feeling her . . . Well. But he was special, certainly nothing
like other men. The prickly heat all over Agnes's face deep-
ened. He suddenly broke the connection and sat back in
his chair, as if snapping out of a trance.

"Your heart," he said to Agnes earnestly. "What is it
telling you?"

"Well, let's see . . ." Agnes was really trying. But this
soul-searching stuff was all new to her, certainly unlike
anything she had encountered in church. "It's not
steady . . . it jumps all over the place . . ."

"Does it cry out?"

"Cry out? What do you mean?"

"Your heart is a fluttering sparrow caught in the barbs
of thorns. It stops its rhythm in hopelessness and confusion, then beats its wings wildly, as if to escape the fowler's
snare."

"Escape . . ."

"Your soul longs to be free, yet equally yearns for love
and security."

This was amazing. Bob was reading the truth about
her, hidden even from herself. The other ladies shifted a
bit in their chairs, wondering with a mingling of hope and
dread if they would be next.

"To cure the body, listen to the soul. You're not
happy in the life you've chosen for yourself, Agnes."

At this the floodgates opened, and Agnes opened her
mouth and began to sob. Ethel wished she'd get a hold of
herself. Annette Jamieson began to rummage loudly in
her black vinyl purse for a Kleenex, mistakenly pulling out
a Tampax, which she shoved back in the bag in mortifica-

tion. Pearl reached over and patted Agnes's hand, almost as a reflex. What she wouldn't give for a good drag on an Export A.

"It's true," she gasped. "Shelton takes so much for granted. He expects me to do everything. He . . . w . . . w . . . won't even marry me. *I want children!*" This primal cry disturbed the women even further. "Hush now," said Pearl. Such things weren't to be spoken of. Childlessness was a tragedy, she knew from personal experience, but women were meant to bear this cross in silence.

"Why do you stay with him?" Annette asked her sharply. "Sounds as if he's taking you for a ride."

"But he's a writer. An artist. He needs support."

"Support, my foot. He needs to get a job and get married like everybody else."

"I can't tell him that. He'd be crushed."

"How old are you, Agnes?" Bob asked gently.

"Thirty-eight."

"So time for fulfilling your dream is running short."

"I never thought of it that way."

"And time runs short in another way for Shelton, as he approaches the end of his life."

"Oh," she burst in, "but Shelton will live a good many more years, I'm sure! Maybe twenty."

"And you'll be—"

"Fifty-eight," Agnes said miserably. Suddenly she hated Bob and his prophecies. It was all a bunch of lies. She began to gather up her things to leave.

"Just think about these things, will you, dear?" Willie Peck's voice was full of concern. Agnes made a sour face and headed for the door. Ethel suddenly emerged from the kitchen in confusion. "Did I miss anything?"

"Goodbye, Ethel," Agnes said flatly, "and thank you very much."

"Oh, are you leaving, dear?" Ethel looked at her in confusion.

"She took things the wrong way," Annette said. "Too personal."

"Oh, I'm sure Bob didn't mean . . ."

"Look, it isn't Bob's fault," said Agnes dully. "My life is nothing. All he did is point that out."

"Agnes!"

"Bob never meant any such thing," Willie piped up defensively. Finally Bob spoke, and the women hung on each word.

"Dear Agnes, of course I meant no harm. But to relieve the distressing symptom you've been experiencing, you need to find the source of the problem. *Are* you happy with Shelton?"

"Happy?" She pronounced the word as if it had a foreign taste.

"Yes, happy."

"I'm not sure if I've ever been happy." The other women did not want to hear this. It made them wonder if they had ever really been happy, either. It didn't bear thinking about. Wasn't it better to just get on with things?

"What does it mean to you, then," Bob pressed on, "to be happy?"

Agnes's sensitive pink face went through a multitude of changes in only a few seconds. These were things she had never stopped to ask herself. It was shocking, both terrible and thrilling.

"I want something of my own." She said it with utter certainty, then realized with a little jolt that it was true.

"And what might that be, dear Agnes?" Bob's voice was translucent with tenderness.

"A baby," she gasped, her face filling with emotion. "Or maybe even a job. I've always wanted to work in a hospital."

"So what's stopping you, Aggie?" Annette asked in her usual direct way.

"I don't know. Shelton doesn't want me to work."

"That's because he wants you around all the time to wait on him." Annette could be harsh, but she had a way of getting to the heart of things.

Then Bob spoke. "Agnes, are you using Shelton as a hiding place? So long as you're with him, you don't need to risk doing anything new and unfamiliar." By this time the women in the group were convinced that Bob was a genius.

"Life goes on in the same old way, year after year. And I don't make any changes. Shelton seems to like it that way."

"Stop spending all day typing his manuscripts for him, then," Annette said. "Get yourself a job at the hospital. Nurse's aide. It's a place to start."

"I don't know if I . . ." She had put her hand to her pounding heart, then realized the significance of the gesture.

"You owe it to yourself, Agnes," Ethel encouraged her. "After all you've done for him. You deserve a life of your own."

Do I have to be the first? Agnes wondered. No one was asking the other ladies to do anything, to make any changes, just her. She felt both important (perhaps for the first time in her life) and unfairly burdened. Resentment vied with a hitherto-unknown pride in herself. It was the queerest mix of feelings she had ever experienced.

"I need to think about it," she said, then added earnestly, "But I *will* think about it. I will. I have to go now. But thank you, Bob. You were wonderful." Then she went out the door with an air of total preoccupation. The other women sat in silence for a moment.

"Tea, anyone?" Ethel asked.

"I would love a cup of tea, Ethel," Bob said.

"Tell me, Bob," Willie Peck asked, "how did you know all those private things about Agnes?"

"I didn't. But she knew them, and I helped her come to the realization of what was in her heart."

"Oh, why don't we learn about these things in church?"

He sighed, closed his eyes a moment, then spoke. "Church is a place to begin, a place to draw together with others in spiritual community. But sooner or later we all must look deeply within ourselves."

"Why does Reverend Sanderson have such a hard time with all this?"

"It's simply new to him," Bob smiled, "as it is for Agnes. New ideas are never easy."

"Read us more from your wonderful book," Willie urged. For some reason she felt about twenty years younger, and she wanted the feeling to last.

"I think you've digested enough for one day. Come, let us partake of Ethel's wonderful baking."

And they broke her wheat germ brownies like the bread of life and partook of dark, steaming cups of Red Rose tea as if it were the Blood of Christ itself.

18.

Whump.

Ta-whump-whump-whump-whump.

Whumpita-whumpita.

Whump!

A bit of plaster twinkled down from the kitchen ceiling and lightly dusted the surface of Aubrey's mug of coffee. He gazed at it glumly. There was nothing wrong with that roof. Aubrey could have fixed it himself. Only a few shingles. Getting someone in was plain foolishness. Then Min had made the phone call.

"Let's get that nice young man in to re-shingle the roof," she piped up on a rainy evening when the usual array of pots had to be arranged under all the drips.

"You don't mean Jesus?"

"Everybody's talking about him, Aubrey. You're so slow to catch on. He's been doing wonders with the church. Haven't you noticed the paint job?"

Yes, he admitted to himself, the church did appear a little less green these days. The usual look of moldy Wonder Bread had given way to a pristine whiteness. Door hinges no longer squealed. Cracked windows were replaced. Even the old hardwood floors shone with a new coat of wax. The place looked cared for, not neglected, for the first time in years. Bob had even refused payment, calling it volunteer work. Nin Sanderson was in a state of total confusion, which did give Aubrey a certain degree of satisfaction.

"But you're paying him too much. Twenty-five dollars. Sweet Jesus."

"It's a full day's work," Min shot back.

"I hear he moved into new digs. What did he do, buy the old Gribble place?"

"It's only a modest apartment. He only had one room before. He's a bachelor. He needs his comforts."

I'll bet, thought Aubrey. He'd heard at Guy's the other day that a gaggle of women had him over for some kind of strange prayer meeting. *A hippie church*, thought Aubrey. *Just what Harman needs*. It was funny, but Pearl seemed to like him. Every time his name came up she defended him. And she quit smoking again, this time lasting more than the usual two weeks. She wasn't as cranky this time either. But Aubrey fervently hoped she wouldn't get mixed up in all this Bob stuff.

"Aubrey." Min's sharp, irritating voice was worse than all the hammering. "The reunion's in only a few weeks. Don't you think we should invite Bob?"

"Since when is he a Connar?"

"He's a friend of the family. Half the town will be there anyway; you know that."

"Yes, for the free food and booze!" Sometimes Aubrey heard the bitter words that came out of his own mouth and wondered exactly when he had become like this, so sour, so cynical.

"We've got seventeen Pedlows coming from Ireland."

"Christ! Why?"

"They're blood kin."

"One nosebleed, and they're off the list." Min got that compressed look that meant she was trying not to laugh. Aubrey knew he had scored a point.

"I didn't think there were seventeen Pedlows left in the world. The blood's got so thin. Look at Eileen. And that girl of hers! I knew something terrible would happen to her when she gave her that godawful Catholic name."

"Love children run in the family," Aubrey remarked nonchalantly, shuffling through an old pile of correspondence. He never threw anything out and the clutter in the old rolltop desk was alarming. All the letters he never had answered.

The back door opened and Bob clattered in, sweaty and dusty, but beaming. "Bob!" Min cried, her voice artificially young and full of adoration, as if he were Maurice Chevalier or something. "Do take a lunch break. Aubrey, make Bob a sandwich."

For the love of Christ, Aubrey thought, *it's ten-thirty in the morning.*

"Thanks, Mrs. Connar, but I brought my own lunch. Macrobiotic."

What the hell?

"Oh, all those bean sprouts and things. Well, that's fine. Aubrey, put on the coffee."

Aubrey reluctantly dumped the remnants of the stale coffee out of the percolator and began to run some water. Bob's searching eyes scanned the kitchen table, then fastened on one of the letters at the top of the pile. His pupils dilated suddenly, hugely. Otherwise he did not allow himself to react. But Min noticed it.

"Sit down, Bob. Make yourself at home." She had a

disgusting smile on her face, which turned all her wrinkles upside-down. Bob sat in one of the cracked green vinyl chairs, his pulse racing, the letter he had written to Aubrey a mere toss away.

So he knew. Or he didn't know. Or knew but wasn't acknowledging him, purposely, to cut him dead. Which was it? Or could it be something else, a selective blindness, even with the evidence staring him in the face? Confusion sickened him and his gut roiled like a trapped octopus, writhing and squirting ink. It was all he could do to look normal, but Min picked up on the veil of anxiety palpitating invisibly all around him. Her bright hooded eyes darted over to the letter on top of the stack.

"So I hear you've started a new church," Min remarked brightly.

"Oh, no, Mrs. Connar, it's nothing like that. Ethel just had a little gathering of friends over at her home. She asked if I'd read some excerpts from some of my books. It was a lovely afternoon."

"Do call me Min."

"Oh—all right, Min. Some of the guests wanted to know more about the principles of healing. I was glad to share with them the little bit that I've learned through my readings and experience."

"I heard you did a miracle." The girlishness creeping into her tone made Aubrey sick.

"I just gave a few practical suggestions which seemed to help. Evan was motivated to change, and Ethel was eager to support him. People heal themselves, Mrs.—Min." He blushed a bit. Aubrey thought: *this shit-eating humility is too much for me.*

"But they can't do it on their own."

"Not always. I'm just there to help things along."

"So when is the next meeting?" Oh, not this, thought Aubrey. Does this mean I have to trundle her all the way over to Ethel's once a week to listen to some hippie?

"I assume it will be at the same time next week. At least, the ladies seemed eager to meet again."

"No men in this group, then," Aubrey broke in as he clattered the coffee-perk. He'd make coffee. Oh, he'd make coffee all right. But he wouldn't do it willingly. In fact, he'd make coffee at them, for revenge.

"Well, no, Mr. Connar."

"Aubrey." He wouldn't have Min one-upping him here.

"Aubrey. So far no men have come to the meeting, but there's nothing to say that they won't in the future."

"Do you take up a collection?"

Bob looked stunned, then smiled, his face a little strained. "You don't need to worry, Aubrey. It's not like that."

"I should say not," Min said, looking scandalized.

"I just thought . . . you know, to cover your costs." There was something oddly familiar about Bob's softly whiskered young face, but he couldn't put his finger on it. Around the eyes? No, he was imagining things.

"There are no costs. Just time, and I'm glad to give it." Bob was starting to look a little uncomfortable. There was a knot of something unfinished in the very air, a tension all three of them sensed but couldn't do anything about: "Well, I suppose I should get back to work now. Shouldn't waste a fine day like this."

"But you haven't had your coffee yet." Min glared over at Aubrey. It was obviously his fault.

"Oh, I don't drink coffee, Mrs.—Min. Ginger infusions are much better for the digestion."

"You mean the powder?"

"No, I'm referring to ginger root."

"Ginger is a root? I thought it was a powder that came in jars. You know, to put in the cookies."

"Well, I must be going." Bob felt about as comfortable as a worm writhing before a pecking bird.

"Don't work too hard," Aubrey threw after him as a parting shot.

"Aubrey," Min snapped the moment the door banged behind him, "you drove that nice boy away with your attitude."

"Attitude? Am I supposed to like hippies now?"

"You made him uncomfortable. Asking if he takes up a collection. I want to go to this meeting, Aubrey. When is it, Tuesday?"

"Wednesday," Aubrey said, then regretted it. He was also a little shocked that he knew. Who had told him? Was it Pearl?

"I need to get out more." Min pulled out her pathetic-old-lady voice, full of Irish self-pity. "I'm practically a shut-in. I need a social life, Aubrey, even if you don't."

"I'm just worried you'll take a fall," Aubrey grumbled. "Break your hip."

"You *do* worry about me, don't you, son."

"I just don't want you bedridden. Bedpan duty doesn't appeal to me."

"He's coming."

"What?"

"To the reunion. Bob is coming."

"Oh, all right." As if I had anything to do with the

guest list, he thought. Appease the old harpy. But he did worry about falls. She wouldn't get a walker because that was for "old crones," she said. A cheat. It was only a matter of time until something happened.

For some reason Aubrey was dying for a cigar. He was only allowed to smoke in certain parts of the house, so he slipped upstairs to his fume-reeking bedroom to sneak the solace of a Muriel.

Min sat for a second—long enough for Aubrey to be out of eyeshot. Then her bluish, dry old hand shot out and nabbed the letter on the top of the stack.

Unfolding it carefully, she held it two inches away from her slack-lidded old eyes and began to read.

19.

Dwight Connar cranked the wheel of his '57 Plymouth station wagon as he turned the corner onto Eagle Street in sunny Harman. God was putting on quite a show that day. The ripeness of summer was palpable, sensual. Quiveringly delicious smells streamed in through the open window—heady, blossomy smells like the sweet throat of a woman warm with desire. Dwight shifted on the hot vinyl bench seat. His balls were stuck to his leg, no doubt due to the constricting, rubberized effect of his snug-fitting dark-purple polyester pants. His wide-sleeved shirt was striped purple and beige—"flocked," with little fuzzy bits all over it that caused Sadie to purse her lips. Stella Alderman had liked it, fingering the flocked parts. "Mod," she had said.

Dwight wasn't exactly sure why he had driven to Harman on this fine July Saturday. Of course it had nothing to do with that mule-headed brother of his. Nothing to do with the reunion either, which Dwight anticipated with a certain gut-squeezing dread. He just felt restless and antsy, literally itchy from the sensuous heat, and had the sudden urge to take a drive.

And here he was in Harman, his hometown. It was only a coincidence that he stopped by Soapy Hudson's lumberyard, just to have a little look around. It being

Saturday, everything was locked up tight. Dwight noticed some funny-looking cigarette butts on the driveway, with twisted ends. Somehow he couldn't picture Soapy smoking "whacky tobaccy," so he figured it had to be some of the local kids.

So they had it here, too. Sooner or later things had to filter down as far as Harman, though it often seemed like the last stop before the end of the world. Somehow there was more freedom in Horgansville, more latitude. And civic pride. Glittery homemade banners were going up everywhere for Horgie Days, and though Dwight had to admit they looked pretty hideous, a palpable excitement was building. Dwight was sorry he'd have to miss the fun.

He poked around in the driveway for a few minutes, then went around behind the office to see if the set-up had changed. He should have known better. Except for the reefers, Harman had been in an air-sealed time lock for the past thirty years. Dwight was starting to bumble back to his car when a large man wearing a wide-brimmed straw hat loomed out from behind the shed, brandishing a hacksaw menacingly in front of him.

"What the hell do you think you're doing?" the figure said.

"Soapy! I knew it was you."

Soapy cautiously lowered the saw. He had to stare for a long moment before the fog in his expression cleared.

"Jesus, Dwight, I didn't even recognize you, you son-of-a-bitch. What've you done to yourself?"

"It's my new look."

"I can see that. You look like one of them damn—"

"Listen, Soapy, I've just come by to say hello. Let's not get into a hassle, eh?"

"Hassle?"

"Yeah, a . . . an argument."

"Jesus, Dwight, I have no bones to pick with you. You know that. It's just that I can't get over the getup."

"How's Alma?"

"Alma? She's—" He gestured vaguely. Alma was Alma, and things didn't vary. "And Sadie?"

"She's—" He made the same vague gesture. It was some sort of code. You asked after each other's wives, but everyone knew the answer didn't really matter.

"How's business?"

"The same. Seen Aubrey?"

"Not in fifteen years. You knew that already."

"I thought it was twenty."

"I'd like to go see Mother. But Aubrey's just taken her over. I can't get to her except through him."

"He's not exactly holding her hostage, Dwight."

"But it's all so awkward. Eileen came to see her, and she and Aubrey got into their usual row. I don't want any—"

"Hassles?" Soapy said, a quizzical look on his face.

"I'm not a hippie, Soap."

"Guess not. But you're sure starting to look like one."

"Some of us move with the times." Dwight immediately regretted saying it. Soapy looked like he was refusing to take offense.

"If the times made any sense," he said with finality, "I'd move with them too." Then, with no parting words, he disappeared again behind the tool shed, swinging the hacksaw. Dwight stood there for a moment, feeling like a complete fool.

He made his way back to the driveway, shaking his

head in confusion. Some homecoming this turned out to be. So far the reception had been less than gracious. As he made to get in the car, someone strode up to him from out of nowhere and came to a dead stop.

"Dwight Connar. It can't be you."

Dwight looked at the man and tried to figure out who the hell he was.

"I'm sorry, I—"

"You don't recognize me, do you?" Yet the man looked oddly familiar, with a resemblance to some minor B-movie actor. His coarse face radiated unintelligence.

"I, uh—"

"I'll give you a hint. I have a famous brother."

Famous. Who in Harman could lay claim to a term like that? Dwight's confusion increased.

"Okay, I'll give you a bigger hint. His first book's being made into a movie next year. They're trying to get Barbara Stanwyck to play the mother."

"Sam Gribble?"

"Call me Shemp. Everybody else does. Jeez, you've lost a lot of weight! You on the Drinking Man's Diet or something?"

"I uh, just started doing these exercises, you know, the Air Force plan—"

"C'mon over to Sid's, and I'll buy you a drink." It was eleven in the morning and this man was already proposing getting soused. "Or are you into that other stuff— y'know—" He gestured at the roaches on the driveway.

Dwight shook his head. "Sadie'd have a fit."

"That why you still have this old junker?" He kicked the front tire of the wagon disdainfully.

"Well, it's practical."

"I'll say. Also falling apart."

Dwight hated to admit even to himself that he lusted after a new car. He'd recently test-driven a Renault in a wild shade called Grabber Yellow and nearly bought it. But that look Sadie could put on—not of anger, but disappointment—caused him to shrink back like a man's privates in cold water.

"Well, I'm afraid I have to go now, Sam—"

"Shemp."

"Oh. Shemp, then. How *is* your brother, anyway?"

Shemp's face cramped a bit. It was a question he had to answer nearly every day.

"Doing all right. Shacked up with a hussy, as usual."

"Really?"

"She's got herself a job now. Perce is having a fit. *Shelton*, I should say."

"What's she do?"

"Cleans up old people's shit."

"Oh." It didn't sound like much of a career. "Well, give him my best."

"I will. I always do." Shemp beetled off, likely to the bar for a quick one. Suddenly Dwight thought of Fry King back home, as he usually did in moments of stress or tension. What he wouldn't give for a good feed of chicken right now, and all the comforting feelings that came along with it. Of course there was no decent chicken in Harman, only that godawful American stuff in the bucket, plastic. But his mouth began to water anyway.

And it was amazing how his old car homed in on the Harman Chicken Villa on Tamarack Drive as if it already knew the way. It wasn't even lunchtime and already the place was swarming with people. It was amazing how lively a dull place could seem. If there was nothing else to be excited about, you got excited about a piece of chicken.

And wasn't that Ethel and Evan McConnaughey sitting at a corner table? Dwight had heard from somebody-or-other that Evan was supposed to be permanently disabled—lumbago or something, wasn't it? What was he doing out of the house? Was that a dog under the table? Dwight tried to pretend he hadn't seen them, but it was too late.

In exact unison, each of them cried, "Dwight! Come join us!" Dwight was surprised to see Evan eating nothing but a huge mound of salad—finely ground green coleslaw, macaroni mixed with finely chopped red sweet peppers, and bean salad swimming in a thin oily dressing. Ethel had removed all the skin from her chicken so that her meal looked denuded and uniformly beige. The dog rose up on its hind legs so that its small thing pointed obscenely upwards. Ethel threw him a piece of skin, which he devoured noisily. Then he began to whine for more.

"So what brings you here after all these years, Dwight?" Evan asked.

"Just having a look around. You know, for old time's sake."

"You look ten years younger," Ethel gushed. "What've you been doing?"

"Air force exercises."

"Is that so!" Evan took a huge bite of coleslaw. "They make the best cabbage salad here," he mumbled through the bulging mouthful.

"You're looking well, Evan. What have *you* been doing?"

Dwight almost wished he hadn't asked. The simple

question unleashed a torrent of enthusiasm, particularly from Ethel. Oh, but hadn't he heard about Bob? Bob was a miracle worker. Bob had changed their lives. Bob had started a new church. It was all a little hard to absorb. Instead of turning water into wine, this Bob had apparently turned raspberry Freshie into a miracle cure. Now he had a growing band of disciples, all women. It was downright bizarre.

"Oh, but you have to invite him to Horgansville sometime, Dwight. He'd do Sadie a world of good."

I'll bet, thought Dwight.

"Well, we're pretty busy right now, what with Horgie Days—"

"But this is something different. This is the life of the spirit. Bob has opened up a whole new world for us." The dog snuffled loudly, licking its greasy chops.

"I'm glad to hear that." Dwight wished only to flee, but reluctantly ordered a three-piece chicken dinner with french fries, a roll, and a tub of spicy gravy. Not a patch on Fry King, but it would have to do.

He sat for the next hour listening to Ethel's monologue on Bob, occasionally throwing in a one- or two-syllable comment as he chewed his chicken with an increasing sense of exhaustion. Already he felt as if he knew Bob intimately. He felt like the man in the Stephen Leacock story who couldn't excuse himself from dinner, slowly expiring from boredom and despair. He wondered if he could kill himself by swallowing a chicken bone, but decided the risk of pulling through was too great. They'd probably call Bob.

After interminable goodbyes and the usual insincere plans to meet again, he got up from the table, his legs a little rubbery. He made his way towards the door, but then stopped in his tracks as if his feet were nailed to the floor.

A middle-aged man sat in one of the plastic booths with a chicken leg in his hand, his mouth open, anticipating the first bite. Their eyes met with a palpable flare of shock, and the man dropped the leg on the table.

"Aubrey," Dwight said.

"Dwight."

Across the room, Ethel and Evan twisted around in their chairs, Ethel pointing to the two men. "Look," she said in a loud stage whisper to Evan. "Look."

20.

There was news in Harman, the kind of news to set tongues clacking. It was all anyone talked about at the bakery or anywhere else, displacing even Min's birthday or Horgie Days or Dwight's sudden appearance at the Harman Chicken Villa, which had left Aubrey shell-shocked. It was hotter, juicier news even than Eileen's daughter's burgeoning pregnancy or the murmurings that Bob Hemphill had blood kin somewhere in the town of Harman. (And who had started that one, anyway—was it Agnes, who'd heard it from Shelton, who'd deduced a few things from Bob's cryptic statements about finding his "roots"?)

"It's hard for me to believe," said Mrs. Wilhelmina Peck to the members of her bridge club on a hot Thursday evening, "that anyone could be so heartless."

"But that mother," Sophie Howland put in. "Sounds like she's not right in the head to begin with."

"Neither is the child," Willie stated. "But it's still no reason to—"

"Maybe she was desperate," Pearl Smith said, surprising everyone. She usually didn't say very much, but since quitting smoking she had a new tendency to speak her mind. "You know. Maybe he was more than she could handle."

"There's places for retarded kids," Edna Purvis insisted. "Like St. Thomas."

"I heard that he ain't exactly retarded," Sophie said. "More odd-like."

"Still," Willie declared, "abandonment is abandonment. It's a gravely serious charge. God alone knows what happened to the child."

"Maybe somebody took him in," Pearl said. They all looked at her in surprise. They had liked the old Pearl better.

"I don't think too many people would want to take in a retarded boy," Edna said.

"But he ain't retarded," Sophie insisted. And so on and on it went, circling back on itself like gossip always does, going nowhere.

Guy at the bakery believed that if half the energy that went into gossip could be funnelled into constructive activity, the problems of the world would soon be solved. These days every other customer asked him, "Hear about that little boy? Quite a shock, eh? Mother's not right in the head. Neither is the kid. What's the world coming to?" Being retarded was a judgement, many believed, a moral shadow never to be overcome. Kids like that should be put away somewhere. For their own protection, of course. It was a shame to see women out in public with children who weren't right—mongoloid, or deformed. Everyone stared; they couldn't help it. Pity vied with revulsion. It was the way things were.

Dot could not help but be aware of all this talk, as she regularly visited Guy's for day-olds. Since Guy was a particularly keen observer of his customers' habits, he noticed a couple of things. First of all, Dot did not comment on the scandal of the abandoned boy. Kept her thoughts to herself, if she had any at all. It was not like Dot to be so reticent. She usually had a thing or two to say. Secondly, she had started to ask for more sweets. Particularly chocolate-flavoured things—brownies, cocoa macaroons. A change in tastes could mean something. In a younger woman of different circumstances, he might even suspect pregnancy; he'd correctly predicted the coming of both of Annette Jamieson's brats when she developed a craving for exotic things like petits fours and madeleines. Dot was too old and too strange to be in that condition, despite rumours of her delinquent past. But what else might a food craving signify? Loneliness? Depression? He hoped it wasn't illness. But Dot, though she'd been acting a little more strange than usual lately, seemed fine—a bit preoccupied, maybe, as if she had some sort of a project going. What could it be? *Damn*, thought Guy. *I'm getting as bad as the rest of them.*

Dot did what was necessary day by day, knowing full well that the time for sharing her home with the odd little boy was growing short. Once he had tripped on a kink in the carpet and bumped his head quite badly, and Dot felt a terrible anxiety, wondering whether he needed to see a doctor. "Gareth," she said to him. "Are you sure you're okay?"

"Head." She cherished his few words, believing they were signs of awareness. The goose egg on his forehead had gone down, and all seemed well. But what if something else went wrong? Had he had his shots? He wasn't going out or mixing with other kids—not that he could, even if he wanted to. So maybe he wouldn't catch the inevitable measles and chicken pox and mumps that periodically did the rounds.

But when you had a child under your roof, it was hard not to think of the future. They were all future anyway, kids were, because they had no past to speak of—unlike Dot, who had already lived away the best part. Being with someone was a pointed reminder of how alone she was all the rest of the time. The cats were a great comfort, and less trouble than people with their incessant expectations and cutting judgements. But a cat wasn't a person. You couldn't hold a conversation with one. Couldn't with Gareth either, for that matter, but maybe that was why she'd grown so comfortable with the boy. He had certain daily needs which she was more than happy to fulfill, but he didn't (because he couldn't) question Dot's strangeness. In fact he didn't even see it. Seldom could she truly be herself with another human being. In its own unlikely way, it was a blessing.

Of course, there was a price to pay—all that secrecy, for one thing, and the haunting, pervasive awareness that this little boy wasn't normal and never would be. Once she had caught him trying to cut his own hair off with the sewing scissors. Then there was the time he had nicked his finger, and she'd found him sitting at the kitchen table, happily dabbling and messing in his own blood as if he were fingerpainting. Whenever he got upset he tried to bang his head on the floor, and sometimes, for no reason, he sat rocking by the hour, completely absorbed by the repetitive motion.

Dot liked to think that Gareth had an inner life, like she did, that no one could ever know about. Strange as his life seemed on the outside, perhaps it was rich inside. She wondered what would become of him, if he would be put away somewhere where no one understood him. Surely things as they were couldn't be any worse for him than that. But she had no illusions that anyone would ever see it that way.

When the doorbell rang one sultry morning, the cats jumped in unison and swarmed towards the stairs. No one ever came to Dot's door. The Fuller Brush man knew better than to deal with the likes of her. Even the postman always seemed in a hurry to get away from the place, as if it were a haunted house. Dot knew that this could mean no good, but trudged to the door anyway. An unanswered bell could only lead to further trouble.

When she saw two well-dressed middle-aged women clutching magazines in front of their chests like armour plating, she got the lay of the land immediately. It was God's Witnesses—"Witlesses," she liked to call them. Not to worry, she'd dispatch them soon.

"Good morning, Ma'am," one of them said, her eyes darting over Dot's layers of clothing. "And how are you this fine morning?"

"Swell."

"We have an important message we'd like to share with you today."

"I'm sure you do."

"Many people are concerned about the decline in moral standards among today's youth."

"Are they?" Already Dot was growing bored.

One of the women fished out a glossy magazine with a picture of a disreputable-looking hippie on the cover. "We believe we have an answer to the teenage drug problem through the power of Mighty Yahweh, as outlined in the current issue of *The Sentinel*."

"But I belong to another religion."

"You do?" the women asked in unison.

"The Hare Krishnas. You know—Hare Krishna, Hare Krishna, Krishna Krishna . . ." She hoped the chanting would scare them away, but they merely looked puzzled.

Then the bun-headed one on the left brightened. "Oh! I see you have a little boy."

Dot was filled with consternation. It was completely unlike Gareth to come up to people, but there he was, standing behind her in the doorway with a ballpoint pen in his hand, idly scribbling all over his face.

"What's his name?" the other lady asked.

"Uh . . ." Dot panicked, afraid for some irrational reason of revealing the name she had given him. "James."

"Hello, James," the bun-head said.

"Hello, James." The two women looked at each other.

"James. Go back inside and wash your face."

"Face," Gareth said, sticking the point of the pen deep into his left nostril.

"You'll have to excuse us. We have to go clean up. Thanks for coming." Dot closed the door on the two, her heart hammering. They must have known she was far too old to be his mother. Grandmother, maybe? She wished she'd done something with her hair before coming to the door, as it was standing stiffly on end all over her head like a grey halo. The short orange paisley muumuu with the pink vinyl zipper down the front probably didn't lend her much more dignity. In fact, she thought, catching a glimpse of herself in the hall mirror, she looked like a psychedelic witch. For just a second, the thought pleased her, but then the panic resumed.

Never mind, she told herself. The Witnesses were so oddball anyway, always forecasting the end of the world and the like, that no one was too likely to listen to them. But for the next few days she was careful to keep Gareth well clear of the door and even the windows. One bright morning as she set out for her usual food run, she propped him in front of the TV, which was blaring out some mindless marionette show called *Supercar*. As she slipped out the front door, Gareth sat staring at the air in front of him, lightly and rhythmically slapping his own face.

She had gotten as far as the end of the walk and was opening the front gate when a young police officer strode up and planted himself in front of her.

"Mrs. Ronald Varley?"

"Dorothy Varley."

"Mrs. Varley, I wonder if you'd care to answer a few questions."

"No, I wouldn't care to. Do I have a choice?"

"It will make matters easier if you do."

Dot sighed, pressing her fingertips into her eyes. She knew that resistance was pointless.

"All right then. You might as well come in. I have nothing to hide." She led him through the front door and was surprised to find that Gareth was no longer on the sofa. He usually stuck where she planted him. She sat the officer down and stood over him, no longer panic-stricken but resigned, almost relieved.

"Were you aware, Mrs. Varley, that a young boy named James McDowell has been missing for the past three weeks?"

"His name is *James*?" Dot's mouth flew open. She wasn't sure if it was a laugh or a sob. Lord, she had given him away without even realizing it.

"Do you have any information as to his where-abouts?"

"First tell me," she said, "what will happen to him. That is, if I do know anything."

"Proper steps will be taken."

"Meaning?"

"The boy will be in the custody of the child welfare authorities until more permanent arrangements can be made."

"They'll put him away," Dot said in a flat voice. She knew the smell of an institution, and they were all the same. She remembered being held down, electrodes applied to her head, the frying jolt, the oblivion. And it hadn't helped, just pushed the nightmare away for a while. "Tell me they won't put him away."

"The boy needs help, Mrs. Varley."

"I know that."

"You know where he is, don't you." The cop's manner was just gentle enough that tears began to form in the corners of her eyes.

"I never meant him any harm."

"Of course not."

"I just thought—I mean, what was the harm in giving him a little something to eat? But I knew he wasn't right. Not like other kids. He sort of lives inside himself. He's different. You know what happens to kids like that?"

The cop knew. He sighed. "I realize you're concerned about him, Mrs. Varley. But the boy needs medical atten-tion. It's for his own protection. Please believe that the courts will keep the child's best interests in mind."

A pause. "I have to trust you, don't I," Dot said.

"Yes, I'm afraid you do."

"Okay then. I'll go get him." She went to look for him in all the usual places, but came up empty. He'd hidden himself as well as any of the cats when they didn't want to be found. When she heard a small sound in the bedroom closet, she saw a pair of bright, unblinking eyes suspended in the gloom.

"Gareth. No—James. James? You're going to have to come with me, sweetie."

"James," he said as he scrambled out of the closet. She took his hand and led him down to the waiting cop, stopping once to bend down and make the sign of the cross on his small white forehead.

21.

Aubrey knew the day was going to turn out sour by the way it started.

"Pinch, punch, first of the month, and no return," Min had shrilled at him that morning, making it worse with her accompanying claw-handed pinch and punch. It was an old family ritual; God only knew where it had come from. The pinch and punch were none too gentle, and as usual the odd greeting left him feeling impotent. "No return," indeed. At least it woke him up to the fact that it was now the first of August, and there were only a couple of weeks left before the big event.

In her own horrid way, Min could be quite efficient. She had arranged everything to perfection, even the flights from Portadown and accommodation at the Elm Street Hotel. Aubrey shook his head at the thought of thirty-odd drunken Irishmen and their kin thundering into his quiet life. It made him cringe. And they all seemed to have names like Padraic and Fionnula and Siobhan, impossible to get your tongue around. On the phone, they sounded like they were from outports in Newfoundland, and Min pretended to know what they were talking about as they garbled away in brogue.

Min was acting funny around him just lately, too,

giving him significant looks, as if she wanted to say something but couldn't quite spit it out. This was worse than her usual abrasive comments.

"Something on your mind, Mother?"

"Of course there is. There's only a couple of weeks left."

"I meant something else."

"Oh. Why would you think that, dear?"

"Because you're boring holes through the back of my head with your eyes, that's why."

"Don't get testy with me. It's just that I worry about you."

"Why?"

"You're . . . so alone in the world."

"But I have *you*, Mother."

"I won't be here forever."

"Not that again."

"You know as well as I do that I'm not long for this world. Sometimes I think you should be more prepared. You know, get your life in order."

"What's that supposed to mean?"

"Take responsibility for your past!" Her outburst jolted him. In a moment of panic he wondered if she'd been going through his papers.

"I've cleaned up my life, Mother. I joined AA. I don't make trouble any more."

"Is that all you can say for yourself? That you don't make trouble? There's a difference between staying out of trouble and doing the right thing."

Min was making even less sense than usual. He hadn't told her yet about running into Dwight, nor about the stilted conversation that had followed. It was civil enough, but supremely awkward and downright physically uncomfortable, stomach-twisting, chest-thudding. It had been impossible for him to digest his chicken. Of course, Dwight had asked after Mother. It was the decent thing to do. They went through the usual round of polite questions—how is Sadie, how is Pearl. Fine, fine. But it had been agonizing. Finally Dwight, whose eyes kept darting toward the door, excused himself, saying, "See you on Mother's birthday." When he left, the relief was huge. But seeing Dwight again, looking so changed and yet so much the same, had given him the strangest feeling. For one thing, he couldn't for the life of him remember what they had fought about, and that was unsettling.

Min's strange comments only rubbed his already-raw nerves with salt. Couldn't a man live in peace? Couldn't he just forget the past if that were his wish? But what he had tried to bury wasn't a corpse. It was a living person with a soul, and enough curiosity or need to write him a letter that he hadn't even taken out of the envelope since he first read it.

So thick was the fog that Aubrey had generated around this subject that he paid no heed to the remarks that were flying around Harman about the mystery of Bob Hemphill's natural father. He figured people just needed a new topic of conversation now that Dot was out of jail.

Scandalous, to put an old woman in prison just for sheltering a lost little boy. True, she was a bit crack-minded, but her heart was good. Aubrey had gladly put up the bail money and told Dot he'd be a character witness if it ever came to trial. "They'd likely suspend the sentence anyway."

"It doesn't matter. I'd do the time. It would be worth it."

When he fled the wrath of Min that afternoon to get himself a couple of butter tarts and a cup of tea at Guy's next door, the usual inane chatter from the coffee-break crowd went on all around him. Aubrey tried hard to ignore it as he puffed on his Muriel.

"Maybe it's Joseph Edelstein."

"You mean the guy with the big black beard?"

"Yeah. Jew, ain't he?"

"And he's got the right name." Guffaws all around. "Except his wife's name ain't Mary. It's Rachel."

"But seriously. If Jesus was your son, then that would make you—"

"The most important man in town!" More guffaws. "You'd get to call the shots. Even make it rain if you wanted to. Or send a plague of frogs."

"And look at it this way. Makes it easy to remember your son's birthday." This struck the crowd as the ultimate in hilarity. Aubrey wished he could stick his fingers in his ears.

Then a clang at the door. A large, majestic-looking dog strode in, followed by the man who would have been Aubrey's brother-in-law if he'd had the guts and the morals to do the decent thing all those years ago. But the rest of the bakery fell quiet, as if in awe. It was the man who had put Harman on the map, the man who was even now squeezing an eighteenth novel out of the frailties of the people he observed all around him.

"Mr. Gramercy," Guy cried in delight. This made the day special. He practically ran over to him with coffee and a meringue. Shelton removed his grey fedora and threw it on one of the Formica tables. It happened to be the table where Aubrey was sitting, and this puzzled him. He barely knew Shelton Gramercy and had no desire to know him any better. Like all writers, he was a strange bird, sucking away at other people's marrow. And dead stuck on himself, pretending not to preen and posture at his book signings, when in truth his head was so far up his own rectum that he couldn't even see the light of day.

"Aubrey Connar." He made it sound less a name than a statement of fact. "I've been wanting to talk to you."

"Shelton."

"When was the last time you heard from Faith Farnsworth?"

The name made Aubrey jump. "Why do you ask?"

"I seem to recall," Shelton said as he settled himself beside Ranulf, "that you and she were quite serious about each other. It was after the war. Saw you together at the pictures once. *It's a Wonderful Life* with Jimmy Stewart and Donna Reed, I think it was."

"And your point?"

"Then Faith just disappeared after that. Went to live with an aunt in Edmonton, everyone said."

"Yes, that's what everyone said."

Shelton leaned forward. "And everyone knows what that means."

"Shelton, if you're trying to dig up dirt about my past, you'd better look well to your own."

"Is that a threat?"

"No. Just a reminder about living in glass houses. But the evidence is all grown up now and living in Toronto, so you can relax."

"I hear he's queer. Must've been from that stepfather of his. Bad influence."

"What business is that of yours?" Aubrey was truly

incensed now and aware that their raised voices were drawing unwelcome attention.

"I'm only trying to warn you. Maybe you haven't put the pieces together yet. He may want something, that's all. He may have a grudge. Maybe he's even after Min's fortune."

"Min's—"

"I'd take care of it right away if I were you. Just clear things up, give him what he wants, and send him quietly on his way."

"Who are you talking about?" Aubrey felt his insides turn to ice.

"The same person everyone else is talking about." He shook his head. "God, but you're a stubborn cuss. Or else plain blind. Remember what Faith looked like?"

How could Aubrey forget? The sweetness of her face, the fine, wavy brown hair, the even white teeth. The heart-breaking blue eyes, and the aura of goodness she carried around with her.

But he did not want to see. Did not want to. He got up from his chair, beyond feeling anything but one primal desire, a desire which had lain sleeping in him for nearly twenty years. Now it was horribly awake, and it led him out the door on a grim trudge to an old sanctuary. It struck him as a kind of solution, a way to be done with the whole thing.

It made no difference at all that for years and years he had attended meetings in the Baptist church basement in which everyone talked about all the ways that drinking had destroyed their lives. Booze had always been his beloved, his personal saviour. The fact that he had been dry for all this time mattered not one iota to him in this,

his hour of need. Like the glory of God, booze was still there after all these years, waiting for him. Cunning, baffling, powerful, and . . . *patient*. He anticipated the blessed numbness creeping down his arms and legs, the drowsy head-spin, the blissful sense that nothing, not one goddamned thing on this earth, mattered any more. The force of the thing had a terrible beauty, like wildfire or earthquake. He walked mechanically towards Sid's Bar and Grill, and when he noticed the "Closed" sign on the door, began hammering on it like a mad thing.

After an interminable wait, Sid bumbled to the door, looking annoyed. "Christ, Aubrey, what do you want? We don't open for another two hours."

"I need a drink, Sid."

"Aw, Aub. Come on, now. Can't you get yourself to a meeting or something?"

"I need a drink."

Sid looked at him for a minute. "Sorry, Aubrey."

"Why not?"

"You never settled up your tab from seventeen years ago. Besides, we're not open yet. Tell you what. Come back in two hours. Then you can have a drink." And he closed the door in Aubrey's face, locking it.

He stood there numbly for a moment, trying to think. Then he remembered the bottle at home, Min's brandy. He retraced his steps robotically, calculating how much was left in the bottle. Not much—just a few ounces, but it would tide him over until Sid opened his doors.

But the bottle wasn't in its usual place in the kitchen cupboard. Aubrey panicked. Did they have any vanilla? He remembered stories told at meetings of people melting down 78 RPM records for the bit of alcohol that was in them. Great, next he'd be chewing on Glenn Miller and Tommy Dorsey. He tore the kitchen cupboards apart looking for the brandy, remembering the scene in *Days of Wine and Roses* where Jack Lemmon destroyed the greenhouse for the sake of a bottle, tearing up trees by their roots.

"Aubrey!" Min cried, shuffling her way into the chaotic kitchen. "What are you doing?"

"Spring cleaning, Mother."

"But it's August."

"I know. Pinch, punch—"

"Aubrey. Don't be impertinent. I know what you're looking for. It's not there."

"What are you talking about, Mother?" He looked like a sheepish boy caught with his hand in the cookie jar.

"Or the vanilla either. I got rid of that, too, to be on the safe side."

"I don't know what you mean."

"You know. I mean . . . you *know*. I can tell. It was only a matter of time 'til you figured it out, even with that mule head of yours. I know you very well, son. It's the only thing that would put you over the edge."

Aubrey had no idea what to say.

"It's not such a terrible thing, Aubrey. He's such a fine young man. Everyone in Harman loves him."

"But what does he *want*?"

"Maybe . . . just to know you. To know who his father is. Is that so much to ask?"

"But I abandoned him."

"You can still put that right."

"He must hate me."

"I don't think he hates anyone."

"I have to go," he mumbled. "I have to go."

"Why don't you go for a nice long walk, dear." Her voice was full of concern. But she was fairly sure he wouldn't go to Sid's now. He just needed some time to think.

Thinking is exactly what he didn't do, as his mind went mercifully blank. He walked for hours, until it was past dark, and dark fell late on these long summer days. And then he walked some more. There was a freedom in being completely unaware of the time.

When he slipped back into the house, he could hear Min snoring. He sank into the chair beside the radio, ready for escape. Soon the room was full of the sounds of Shep Fields and his Rippling Rhythm Orchestra. Aubrey sank into it, carried back, back.

The phone rang, jolting him out of a light doze. He answered it, expecting the drunken old lady wanting to talk to Gunther.

"Aubrey."

The voice made his flesh creep with its husky familiarity. The rippling music in the background made him feel giddy and unreal. "Who is this?"

"Do right by your son," the voice said.

"*Father?*"

"Do right by your son. Before it's too late." There was a click, and the line went dead.

22.

In another living room not so far away, another phone was ringing. Not a prankster, not a ghost this time, but a man whose voice was tight with concern.

"Bob Hemphill, please," he said tersely over the fuzzy long-distance line.

It took him a minute to figure out the voice. "Dad?"

"You don't sound like yourself, son."

"You don't either." An awkward pause. "How did you get my number?"

"Your mother still keeps in touch with folks in Harman. It wasn't that difficult." Another pause, which seemed to go on forever.

"I'm okay, Dad."

"I was pretty sure of that," he said, a tinge of weariness creeping into his voice. "You'd let us know if you were in any trouble out there."

"Meaning, if I needed money. Dad, I have a job now. You can relax."

"It's not the money, son. Look, I'm not sure why you've made this pilgrimage or whatever you want to call it. I figure you must have reasons of your own. But you left an awful mess behind you here, and I wanted to remind you of that. You have certain responsibilities."

"What possible good can I do by staying around? We're not getting married. I think we've made that clear. Sally's made her choice already about the baby. I'm sure she'll do fine. She's very capable."

On the other end of the line, Ronald Hemphill blew a long sigh. "So she'll keep the baby, and you'll get off scot-free. I wouldn't be too angry with that so-called 'real' father of yours. It doesn't look like you're handling things any differently."

The realization hit Bob full-force and he fumbled for a cigarette. He had been trying in vain to quit since he landed in Harman. It just didn't look good to the community. After weeks of abstinence, the cravings were agonizing. He sucked on the Winston hungrily.

"Dad," he tried to explain, "I know you're my father, the only father I've ever had. And I know I've been trouble. I appreciate the way you and Mum have stood by me."

"We worry about your health, your mother and I."

"Look, it's been nearly two years since—" He couldn't say it. "I'm better now, Dad. I don't need the pills any more."

"But the doctor said—"

"I don't believe in doctors. People heal themselves." The cigarette was already half-smoked. He shook his head in disgust. "It was just a phase I was going through. You know . . . growing pains."

"Yes, but don't forget that those growing pains left you with a criminal record."

"Not that again. Look, it was just a stupid mistake I made on a dare. I wanted to see if I could make it up to the top window. Then I just sort of climbed in and started looking around . . ."

"I've heard the story. That doesn't explain how that fellow ended up in the hospital."

"It was self-defense." The cigarette was gone and Bob craved another. Panic seized him. Ever since he'd come to Harman he had felt such a delicious sense of freedom, as if he had slipped a noose. Now responsibility threatened to strangle him. He didn't hate his adopted father and had no desire to replace him. But the desire to *know* was a terrible need in him, too long denied.

"So have you met your 'real' father?"

"We've . . . met. I don't think he knows who I am."

"Maybe it's better to leave it that way. Think how you'd feel if Sally's kid caught up with you after twenty years."

"I never thought about it that way."

"I know you didn't. Look, son, you're a decent young man. Everybody used to say so. But you've got some problems you have to face. Running won't solve anything."

"But I've got to find out what I was meant to do with my life."

"Can't you do that here?"

"I love this place, Dad. I feel like I'm doing good work here. You know I need a sense of purpose. And the people are great. They've accepted me for what I am."

"I'm sure they have. You're a charming young man. But what do they really know about you? Doesn't that ever bother you?"

"I just . . . keep busy. I've been fixing up the church."

"Church! We could never get you to go."

"I've started this little group . . ."

"Now son, you know how that turned out last time."

"This is different. A group of older women, nice people.

Churchgoers. Absolutely no drugs, not even pot. Just readings and meditations."

"Just don't get any of them pregnant!"

"Dad . . ." There was real anguish in Bob's voice.

"I'm sorry, son. That was a mean thing to say."

Bob's face contorted. "No . . . it was fair." He took a deep, shivering breath, then let it out. "Look, I'll come home. I promise. I just need to stay 'til . . ." He swiped his hand across his eyes. "'Til my grandmother's birthday. I want to be there."

"Is she the one with all the money?"

"This has nothing to do with money."

"Sorry, Bob. I know I've been rough on you, but I always felt we should speak plainly with each other. You know I always accepted you as my own."

"But I'm not," he said, his voice raw and shaking. "I'm not."

"I don't know what more I can say to you, son."

"Just tell me who I belong to."

A silence. It seemed to last forever. Then his father spoke.

"Maybe," Ronald Hemphill said, "maybe you're God's."

Bob felt as if his chest had been shot out. He hung up the phone with shaking hands and dashed to the bathroom. He'd had the bottle of Lithium for a long time now and hadn't taken any. He poured all the pills into his hand and looked at them. Probably it wouldn't be enough. Then he pictured himself throwing them into the toilet and watching them swirl down into oblivion.

But he didn't. He put them back into the vial, replaced the cap, and set it back in the medicine cabinet next to the jumbo-sized bottle of Vitamin C.

23.

The next meeting of the Church of Bob was considerably more subdued, though none of the ladies could put their finger on exactly why. The air just didn't sparkle as it usually did, even though Bob was as polite and respectful as always. There were two new members out that week: Alma Hudson, a real surprise as she so seldom left the house, and Sophie Howland from Willie Peck's bridge club. Pearl Smith was noticed for her absence, much more than if she had actually been there. Some sort of trouble with Aubrey, apparently, though Aubrey was an old grump even at the best of times.

Agnes popped up out of her chair and called the meeting to order. "Should I read the minutes of our last meeting?"

"That won't be necessary, Agnes," Bob said a little wearily. "Let's just go right into the prayer." Bob would have been happier without all this ritual and structure, but the ladies had insisted on it: "Oh, but we must have an opening prayer!" they said. "Let's do something from that marvelous book of yours."

In unison the group began to chant:

"'Your joy is your sorrow unmasked. The deeper that sorrow carves into your being, the more joy you can contain.

Is not the cup that holds your wine the very cup that was burned in the potter's oven? And is not the lute that soothes your spirit, the very wood that was hollowed with knives?'"

Alma and Sophie looked at each other, a bit confused. This was certainly not like any prayer they had ever heard before. Wasn't The Lord is my Shepherd or the plain old Lord's Prayer good enough for them? And it all seemed so strange. Joy was joy and sorrow was sorrow. Everyone knew they weren't the same thing at all.

"'When you are joyous, look deep into your heart and you shall find it is only that which has given you sorrow that is giving you joy. When you are sorrowful look again in your heart, and you shall see that in truth you are weeping for that which has been your delight.'"

Bob was amazed at how assiduously the women had memorized their lines, as if in school again and learning "O I have slipped the surly bonds of earth," or "In Flanders Fields." He noticed they were all wearing their little silver star pins, like something from CGIT. Ethel had seen them on sale at the Metropolitan and bought a dozen of them as a badge of membership. Bob tried to be patient, knowing they did it out of enthusiasm.

Having become heartily sick of Gibran after weeks of repetition, he decided to expose the women to some meatier stuff and picked up his worn volume of Yeats. At first it went well: his reading of *The Lake Isle of Innisfree* melted them all, leading to exclamations of "Oh, Bob, that was *lovely*," which grated on him a bit. Not that it wasn't lovely, but couldn't they find more eloquent terms? Then he read *When You are Old*, noticing the familiar brightening of the women's eyes from unshed tears.

"'And bending down beside the glowing bars

Murmur, a little sadly, how love fled
And paced upon the mountains overhead
And hid his face amid a crowd of stars.'"

"Oh, that was . . ." Agnes said.

"Tell me," Willie Peck wanted to know. "Why does he say 'a crowd of stars'? That's such an odd expression."

"Maybe it's a misprint," Sophie put in. As a new member, she so wanted to contribute to the discussion.

"That's it. I'll bet it was '*crown* of stars.' What do you think, Bob?"

I think Yeats knew what he was doing, he thought, then felt a bit ashamed of himself for his testiness. Why should they suddenly appreciate this sort of poetry when they had never been exposed to it before? To the ladies he said, "Poets often use unusual turns of phrase. It's so we won't always know what to expect."

"I knew it," said Agnes. "Crowd of stars. *Crowd* of stars. Sounds exactly right to me. You just have to think about it." The women found it a little irritating that Agnes had taken to wearing her new pink uniform to the meetings, but then she was proud of her job as a nurse's aide in the Harman Home of Rest.

"At least," Alma said, "these poems rhyme. They make some sense, not like all this modern stuff."

"Oh, I know, it's terrible," said Ethel. "Not proper poetry at all."

"Well, you see, this is it," Willie chimed in. "That's why our creative writing group didn't last. These young women kept writing poems that didn't even rhyme. Blank verse, they called it. And that stuff they read out loud! Some hotshot new poet. Irving somebody, Irving Peyton, Irving Blayton . . ."

"Layton?" said Bob.

"Yes, that's the one. Does he make money doing this?"

"Poetry isn't always meant to soothe or comfort. Sometimes it's written to unsettle or disturb." He flipped over a few pages in his book. For a moment he wondered if he dared. Was it too great a leap for them? Then he took a breath and began to read.

"'Turning and turning in the widening gyre

The falcon cannot hear the falconer;

Things fall apart; the centre cannot hold;

Mere anarchy is loosed upon the world,

The blood-dimmed tide is loosed, and everywhere

The ceremony of innocence is drowned . . .'"

A dense silence hung over the group as Bob brought the grave, chill work to its completion.

"My, my," said Willie finally, because somebody had to say something.

"What was that one called, Bob?" Agnes asked, eager to understand.

"'The Second Coming.'"

"Sakes," said Ethel.

It made them uncomfortable. Wasn't the Second Coming supposed to be a joyful thing? Or was it really like it was in the Book of Revelation, the one they never used in church? They looked at each other in bewilderment.

"Read us some more from *The Prophet*," Ethel suggested.

"Ladies," Bob said, rubbing his eyes. "The time has come for me to break some news to you that will have an impact on the future of the group. For a lot of very complicated reasons, I'm not going to be with you for very much longer."

For one awful second, Agnes thought he was going to die and could not suppress a gasp. All the women suddenly thought uncomfortably of the gospel scene in the upper room.

"Bob, you're not leaving us," said Ethel, a statement rather than a question.

"Soon I'll be moving on. My reasons are many, but please try to understand that this is something I have to do. What's more, the spirit of this group can continue without me. In fact, nothing would make me happier."

The women were completely unprepared for this shock. No one knew what to say.

"Bob," Ethel finally spoke, "we realize you have to make your own decisions. You're young, and let's face it, Harman isn't a very exciting place to live. But we need you here. We need your guidance. You've changed people's lives in this town."

"Have I? I think I've just offered a few healthy suggestions that happened to come at the right time."

"But you healed my cat!" Agnes's eyes were turning pink.

"Cats have an amazing way of coming back from injury. That's why they say they have nine lives."

"But who will guide the group once you're gone?" said Willie.

"Would it make you feel better if I appointed a successor?"

The women nodded vigorously.

He looked about the room, his blue eyes clear as a lake. They rested on each woman in turn. Then he turned his gaze back to one in particular. Her pupils dilated.

"No."

"Yes."

"You've picked the wrong person. I mean, I'm only . . ."

"Yes, it's you. It couldn't be anyone else. Remember what Reverend Sanderson said in church last Sunday, about Jesus appointing Peter as his successor? 'On this rock I will build my church.' And he picked not the most upright man, or the most flawless, but the most sincere."

"I'm . . ." She was completely overwhelmed. But all the other women began to spontaneously applaud.

"Stand up, Agnes. I pass on the spirit of this little group to you, my friend. And I give these books over into your keeping."

"Oh, but I couldn't take these."

"Yes, I insist. It's for the good of the group." Agnes reluctantly took them, looking stunned.

"You must be very proud, my dear," Ethel said.

"Oh, I'm . . . I don't know what to say." In truth she wanted to run away and hide. Of course, she had to do what Bob said. But the responsibility was overwhelming. Not for the first time, she wondered if being in this group was such a good idea. It led to such . . . upheaval. Shelton was not happy at all about her job, and, in particular, was miffed about the fact that she salted away all of her earnings in a separate savings account. "Getaway money," Shelton grumbled to himself, aware that he'd soon be on the lookout for a new companion, one with less ambition this time. Since starting in this group of Bob's, Agnes had become much more outspoken and no longer did Shelton's bidding immediately. Sometimes she even told him to get his own beer or answer the door himself, so he'd have to deal with the encyclopedia salesman or the

Avon lady. It was stressful, and interfered with his work, a novel about a strange young man with mysterious powers who seduces all the women in Elmsdale.

As Agnes walked home after the meeting, her heart still pounding like the sparrow caught in the fowler's snare, she wondered about the direction of her life, her future. This living with older men was beginning to grow stale, and the relationships always seemed to end badly. For the first time in years she pondered the possibility of living on her own. She had a modest income now, and a nest egg inherited from her father's estate. If she lived frugally, might she not be able to manage? The thought terrified and exhilarated her all at once. But didn't she owe it to Bob to live on her own terms? Once he had left them, there had to be some proof that he had made a difference. Agnes wanted to be that proof.

When she came in the front door and plunked her armload of books down on the dining-room table, Shelton peered at the titles suspiciously. "Awfully heavy reading material for you, isn't it, Agnes?"

"Not any more. These are my books now."

"Are you feeling well, my dear?"

"Never better. But Shelton . . ." She tried to get her thudding heart to slow down, and realized that she had to go ahead and make the leap. "We have to have a talk."

24.

The morning of August 15 dawned sheeny and bright as a freshly minted 1968 penny as Herb Ritter strolled along Electric Avenue to have a look at the floats. Today was the shuddering climax of several days of town revelry, and he'd be damned if he'd let some old bat's birthday upstage the crowning event—his parade. Everyone was involved, from the Brownies to the Kiwanians to the Zonta Club, entering appropriately modelled floats. Even the Spiritualist Society had entered a strange abstract thing that was supposed to represent the Cosmos, but looked more like an extra-large pizza with all the toppings. But these Herb walked past with merely a glance. It was "his" float he was looking for, and when he saw it his heart began to beat a little bit faster.

There, looming in front of him in majesty and awe, was a 15-foot creation which symbolized the essence of the celebrations. It was Horgie the Squirrel, official town mascot and symbol of the industrious nature of the community. In its papier mâché paws the squirrel held a nut the size of a cannonball.

"Beauty," Herb murmured.

Horgie Days had been a tonic for Herb. Though he never complained and was constitutionally incapable of anything like depression, life had gone a tad sour lately, what with losing Eileen. There was no big quarrel, just a growing chill that finally split them apart.

He had thrown himself into Horgie Days like a man possessed, and so far it had paid off. Never had the town spirit been higher. He was almost certain that people in Horgansville would ignore Min's birthday. Oh, those Connars would go, because they had to. But maybe it was just as well. For the rest, he had no worries. Leading the parade would be a special Guest of Honour, none other than the renowned Bobby Gimby, crown prince of the Centennial and composer of the new national anthem, "Ca-na-da (one little, two little, three Canadians!)." Let Harman top this! Oh, he'd heard about the giant throne covered in bile-green crepe paper shamrocks that a team of workmen had erected in the exact centre of Gribble Park. There Min would hold court, waving gently like Queen Elizabeth on a royal tour. Fine. Let her wave. *He* had Bobby Gimby, and he couldn't imagine anyone more exciting than that.

The celebrations had had an almost magical effect on the townsfolk, who had smartened themselves up, dressing in their best. Even Hank Ritter had managed to put together six weeks of abstinence, enough for the stink of booze to exit his pores so that he could make animal balloons for the kiddies. "Remember the hind legs," Herb warned. (Though he hadn't told his brother, Hank planned to slip away midday to make an appearance at the Connar reunion in full Happy Hank regalia.)

Over in Harman, Min was stirring early, shuffling around in the kitchen, trying to get her own breakfast. Aubrey bumbled in wearing baggy, wrinkled pyjamas.

"Mother, for God's sake, it's 5:30 in the morning."

"Oh, I couldn't sleep, dear. I feel like a girl."

You don't look it, Aubrey thought. "Just don't strain yourself, Mother. It's going to be a long day."

"You never thought I'd live this long."

"What makes you say that?"

"Everything. But once I die, things will change. Are you prepared for that?"

"For Christ's sake, Mother, this is your birthday, not a wake." Aubrey took a Muffet out of the box and poured a quarter-cup of sugar over it, drenching it with milk.

"I do hope everyone will wear green," Min said, pouring her Pep flakes.

"Wouldn't orange be more appropriate?"

"I just want everyone to join in the spirit."

"Let's hope no Catholics show up. You could have quite a bloodbath."

"Aubrey, you're always so grim." A beat. "When are you going to talk to Bob?"

"Mother!"

"It has to happen, dear. You know, and he knows that you know. It's ridiculous not to acknowledge the truth."

"What the devil am I supposed to say to him?"

"You'll think of something." She could be so cryptic sometimes, almost Buddha-like. It was maddening. And just try to get it out of her who she'd invited to be the Guest of Honour today. All she would say is, "He's bigger than Bobby Gimby." A rumour was spreading that it was Pierre Trudeau, the "fag Frenchman" to some of the men, and "that divine man" to the women. Could you imagine Lester Pearson or John Diefenbaker having sex? The thought was repulsive. But to be in Pierre's arms . . . ooh, la-la!

The guests had been arriving for several days now, and Aubrey had grown accustomed to all the Irish babble. One of them was a particular nuisance—a tweedy middle-aged pipe smoker named Cormac, who wanted Aubrey to take him on a tour of Harman as soon as he arrived. *I can see it now*, Aubrey thought. *Here's the fire house . . . here's the bar . . . here's the town hall. We're done.* Cormac took an inordinate amount of pleasure in each and every insignificant landmark. The life-sized sculpture of a Holstein outside the Lakewoods Dairy particularly caught his interest, and he climbed out of the car to take several pictures. "Now, Aubrey, stand next to the cow. A little closer. That's it! Now smile." He was absolutely enthralled by the bakery, and bought a dozen currant scones for no reason Aubrey could think of. Maybe he thought it was Irish soda bread.

Speaking of food, Min had considered having the affair catered until the ladies of the UCW, a formidable team, insisted on doing the meal themselves. The pungent smells of boiled corned beef and the gaseous reek of cabbage wafted out of the kitchen of St. Andrew's United as the women bustled about. Everything was perfectly organized and coordinated after years of practice putting on dinners for every conceivable occasion in the church. The men seemed to think that these meals appeared by some sort of fairy magic, but the sweat on these women's brows belied that thought.

In the past few days, Aubrey had become used to seeing a lot of people who looked like Eileen. There were so many of them, and he could never keep all their names straight. The grandchildren were even more confusing. Min had taken to calling them all "dear," and covering her memory blanks with, "Oh, bless his heart." But she was genuinely glad to see everyone, if a little overloaded.

Bernadette had taken a bit of getting used to. Never had Min seen a girl more hugely pregnant, and less ashamed of the fact. That was the thing: the lack of shame. She stuck her belly right out in front of her, and in her day Min had stayed in the house and worn a corset. Never mind that Bernadette really had no choice. The baby was out there, and there wasn't much point in trying to hide it. But she had this habit of wearing very thin cotton tie-dyed shirts that strained across the front. You could even see movement in there, a struggling leg or thrusting hand. It didn't bear thinking about.

"It'll be a girl," Cormac Pedlow said, patting her belly fondly. "You're carrying high."

"How do they know the difference?" Bernadette wanted to know. "I mean . . . does a girl that's not even born yet know enough to sit high like that?"

"Just an old wives' tale," Aubrey said. "Personally, I think it's twins."

"No, there was only one heartbeat. The doctor listened to my tummy the other day. Then I got to listen to it for a minute. It was incredible."

"Bernadette!" Min was scandalized. "Do we need to know all that?"

"Honestly, Gran, you're in the dark ages," she answered. *So disrespectful! So much like her mother at that age! And this girl wasn't even married.*

Today Bernadette was in a green tie-dye shirt so garish it looked like it had exploded in several places. In spite of yet another dead-ended romance, Eileen felt happier than she had in months. ("Why'd you break up with

Herb?" Bernadette had wanted to know. "I don't love him," she said. Bernadette was incredulous. "Is that all?")

At last, the family was coming together again, even if by force. At least they seemed willing to be in the same place at the same time for a few hours. She noticed Aubrey talking to Dwight, and even saying a few words to Barlow. At one point they had shaken hands, astounding her. Were things beginning to turn?

As Eileen drove Bernadette to Gribble Park that morning, her heart lifted with such buoyancy that she felt she could open her throat and sing.

25.

Shelby Davison got out of his car and approached the massive green throne in the centre of Gribble Park. Empty, so far; the woman of the hour had yet to arrive. Poor Gran. She was really getting on in years, ninety years old, the dear. It had been worth it to make the drive from Toronto to be with his own. Though the thought almost made him laugh. Mother was really the only one who accepted him as he was. The rest treated him like some sort of separate species. They said things like, "Well, let him do his thing"—whether they meant it or not—as if it had been his decision. But how much choice did he have in the matter? You love who you love. It was more God's business than his. He knew it, and Mother seemed to know it, and the rest eyed him askance, no doubt relieved that he lived at a safe remove in the big city.

Though Min hadn't yet arrived, the place was abustle. He heard the primitive, blood-stirring sound of a fiddle and a drum—that aggressive, ballsy Irish drumming that had caused so much trouble over the years. The fiddler, who looked to be older than Min, had been imported from Tillsonburg and played his instrument with a kind of gut-deep instinct that had never known the restrictions of notation. One after another he reeled them off—*The Flower of*

Donnybrook, The Wind that Shakes the Barley, Molly Brallaghan, and *Shule, Shule Agrah.* A group of middle-aged women and one lone man in Irish costume were practicing dance steps, stopping every few minutes to chatter with each other. A strange-looking man in a long cape suggestive of Mandrake the Magician swept by, answering the question of what Nin Sanderson did on his day off.

Kids were running everywhere, already starting impromptu games and races on their own, and groups of adults stood around in knots, chatting in an intimate way that shut out strangers completely. Shelby felt as awkward as he generally did at these things. It was a relief to see the familiar faces of Eileen and Bernadette as their car pulled up. He could not believe the size of his sister as she heaved herself out of the car.

"Shelby!" Eileen cried, practically running into his arms. No one ever called him that any more. ("Girl's name, girl's name," he remembered from school.) They hugged hard, and Eileen planted a tangerine kiss-mark on his cheek. Then he smiled at Bernadette.

"Hello, sis."

"Hi, Shell. Staying out of trouble?"

"Doing better than you, obviously."

"You're just jealous 'cause *you* can't have one."

"Stop it, you two. I want this day to be *perfect.* Now I want all of you to get together in one place to represent this branch of the family. There's going to be speeches."

"How are you going to manage that?" Shelby asked.

"She hired a sheepdog. You know, a herding animal."

"Bernadette. *Enough.* Now let's see . . . eleven of us, plus all the children . . . that'll make . . ."

"How many grandkids are there, anyway?"

Bernadette said. "Has anyone ever counted?"

Eileen looked slightly annoyed. "Fourteen."

"Fifteen," Shell threw in. "Don't forget there's one *in utero.*"

"Mum, we can't just stand around all day 'til everyone gets here. Why don't we all meet at two o'clock at the bandshell or something? Oh look, here comes Gran. God, look at the getup!"

"Don't say anything," Eileen whispered as Min made her entrance on Aubrey's arm. She tried not to register alarm, though the shrieking green costume nearly knocked her eye out. For that was what it was, a costume, not a dress. God only knew where she got it. The tight-fitting bodice was covered in flashing emerald sequins, and the skirt with its layers of petticoats flared out diaphanously like the gown of Glinda Goodwitch in the *Wizard of Oz.* She was as heavily made up as Barbara Cartland, and it looked like Mildred Ball from Parisienne Coiffures had made a house call, perming Min's grey straggle into puffy mauve perfection.

In short, she looked like an ancient chorus girl from an amateur production of *Finian's Rainbow,* which was, no doubt, the effect she had been after anyway.

"Mother, your dress is lovely," Eileen said, while Aubrey rolled his eyes skyward. At least he had put on a dark suit and a tie with a tiny bit of green in the pattern, his only concession to Min's dress code.

"Happy birthday, Gran," Shelby said with real warmth in his voice.

Min drew back a bit. "Is that you, Shelley? Sheldon?"

"Just call me Shell." Min accepted his kiss. "You look wonderful."

"Well, I guess *you'd* like it."

"Mother!" Eileen was mortified.

"It's okay, Mum. It's her day. She can say what she likes."

"*Now* he's making sense," Min sniffed as Aubrey helped her up on to her throne. A crowd of well-wishers pushed forward to shake her hand; many had brought gifts, which touched her. Moist-eyed, she unwrapped boxes of Laura Secord chocolates and record albums by Carmel Quinn. Ethel McConnaughey had bought her an exquisite silver bracelet set with delicate shamrocks in Connemara marble. "It's too much," Min said, a little overwhelmed. "No, wear it, Min, wear it. There's a dear. It looks lovely." "No, it's too good for me." "Nonsense. It's just right." She clasped it around her sequinned wrist. "I only wish Melville were here to see it," she sighed.

Shelby wandered off, weaving his way through the little groups of rehearsing baton twirlers, jugglers, and dancers. The mellifluous sound of Irish pipes filled the air, sweet and mellow as a French horn. "Now *those* are bag-pipes," he heard someone in the crowd remark. "Not like those godawful Scotch ones. I'd sooner listen to a vacuum cleaner." The children had already been marshalled into a sack race, and Shell noticed Shemp Gribble joining in, to general hilarity. When the bottom tore out of his sack, they laughed even harder. Now he won every race merely by running. "I always was pretty good in the sack," he quipped.

Shelby was glad he'd come. For the first time in his life, he had a sense of his roots. As oddball as he felt at this gathering, it was reassuring to know he had blood kin here. He was just about to join in a lively game of dunk-the-clown when he saw the back of a head in the crowd that looked familiar.

It looked familiar because it was exactly like the back of his own head. When the man turned, Shell recognized him from the innumerable dust-jacket photos he had seen over the years. For Shell had read every one of the Elmsdale novels, formula-driven and predictable as they were, hoping to find some hint of himself. He had always come up empty.

Shelton Gramercy turned away again, pretending not to know who he was. Shell was about to let it go, just another of the endless slights he'd had to endure all his life, when something in him rose up and spoke.

"Shelton Gramercy." He amazed himself by grabbing the man by the shoulder so that he couldn't get away. For a second he resisted, then turned around.

"This is awkward," Shelton said.

"Not half as awkward as it is for me."

"Then why bother with it? The past is done."

"Aren't you the least bit sorry? Haven't you ever wondered about me?"

"You had a father. A decent home. You did all right."

"Did I?"

"That's what everyone said."

"And you believed it."

"Look, if it's money you want . . ."

Shell looked shocked. "Is that all you can think of? Look, don't apologize to me then. You'd be wasting your breath. Go to Mum. Tell her you're sorry for ruining her life."

"I never did anything of the sort." But Shelton Gramercy was extremely uncomfortable. His eyes shifted and he looked as if he wanted to physically flee. "Eileen would never speak to me anyway."

"You'd be surprised how forgiving she is. But never mind. You're right. The past is gone. I leave you to the life you've made for yourself." Then Shell walked away.

And for the first time in more than seventy years, Shelton Gramercy surveyed his long and productive life and felt it turn to ashes before his eyes.

26.

From the very beginning there had been problems with the squirrel. Something wrong with the design, obviously. Maybe it was just too tall, or weighed too much. "She's not balanced right," Salem Alderman said to Herb, who was close to the breaking point. (He was just trying to be helpful. Herb didn't have to glare at him like that.) Cracks had formed in the squirrel's body and it wobbled dangerously on its base. "Better leave her be," said Salem.

"Over my dead body," muttered Herb. Meanwhile Bobby Gimby and his band were getting restless, looking at their watches. They had another gig in Lambeth that afternoon and had to keep to their schedule. Herb rushed around, offering reassurances in every direction. As the float slowly rolled forward, there was a terrible groaning sound. It had only moved half a block when the great nut fell from Horgie the Squirrel's paws and beaned Herb squarely, sending him sprawling to the ground.

A group of scruffy-looking kids standing nearby bent over in convulsive laughter as the band members, still clutching their cornets and drums, rushed over to help. Herb sat up, a trickle of blood running down his face. "I'm all right, I'm all right. Just get the fucking thing rolling."

So Horgie the Squirrel was launched, cracks and all, and soon the air was alive with the machine-like *whumpa, whumpa, whumpa* of a parade. Back in Harman, Min's great day was ripping along. No fights had broken out, in spite of the gallons of beer served in the refreshment tent. The Irish dancers had been such a hit that the whole audience joined in, a seething mass of flailing arms and legs.

And then the band began to play a waltz. Eileen was standing there, wistfully watching Shelby dance with the near-to-bursting Bernadette, when she felt a light touch on her arm.

She turned around. She became conscious of a subtle, warm, quite wonderful smell. How could she place it? Tweed . . . heather . . . shaving lotion . . . no, don't let this happen again!

"Eileen Connar?"

"You're Cormac Pedlow." She surprised herself by blushing deeply, like a girl. "I'm so glad to meet you. I've been hearing so much about you."

"May I have this dance?"

"Of course."

Pipe smoke, Irish setter, wood pencils . . . what was that smell? Apples, oak leaves . . . Her head swam. She was far too old for this kind of nonsense.

Cormac's blood thundered in his veins. By God, but she was beautiful! Ripe, sweet, full of laughter and the pleasure of living, the woman he had dreamed about for all of his days. It had been worth the trip to Canada just for this moment.

Meanwhile the squirrel made its wobbling way along the main street of Horgansville, lasting a full six blocks before its head fell off. There was nothing anybody could do but keep on moving, while everyone in the crowd joined in the sprightly chorus:

"North, South, East, West,
There'll be happy times,
Church bells will ring, ring, ring."

Never mind that the one-hundredth anniversary of Confederation had been a full year ago. The song was too good to retire. The crowd's enthusiasm was not even dampened when it began to rain. Herb panicked. A cracked squirrel was one thing, but a wet squirrel? A hundred pounds of soggy papier mâché toppling into the crowd? He could be charged with manslaughter. Well, at least criminal negligence. But the juggernaut moved relentlessly forward, the snaking blocks-long line of majorettes and silver-clad Palomino horses and juggling clowns.

Cormac Pedlow strode up to the podium in the Harman bandshell to introduce the speakers. By now everyone was in a glowing mood. Min had had several glasses of sherry and kept bursting into theatrical Irish tears at the slightest provocation. Cormac called Mayor Danville up to the microphone for his opening remarks. Bernadette, leaning against the main pole of the refreshment tent, suddenly jerked herself upright.

"Oh, *shit!*"

"Shh, Bernadette. Language."

"I just pissed myself, Mother!"

"You didn't."

"I can't make it stop." Eileen's heart surged. The crotch of Bernadette's flared maternity jeans was darkening with fluid. "Sweet Jesus," said Eileen.

"Oh no-o-o," said Bernadette, losing her composure completely. Eileen hustled her into the refreshment tent, where a few boozy old men sat swilling down beer. "Clear out, all of you!" she barked, and they practically ran out the door. "Bernadette, do you feel any pain?"

"Oh no-o-o," she wailed, doubling over. It couldn't come this way. First babies took hours and hours. "It's coming!" she cried. "I can feel its head!"

"Quickly!" Eileen grabbed one of the old men as he tried to escape. "Get Dr. Bliss."

"He ain't here yet."

"Get somebody then, anybody! A nurse! Or—is Bob here?"

"Bob who?"

"The one who looks like Jesus."

"Oh, him. Yeah, I think so."

"Go get him. *Now!*" Eileen spread a paper tablecloth on the ground and helped Bernadette lie down. When she pulled down her jeans, she noticed great thick blobs of dark blood and mucous. Her pulse sang in her ears and she thought she was going to faint. Meanwhile, a curious crowd was gathering at the door of the tent.

"Oh, *piss* off, all of you!" Eileen snarled, jerking the flap closed. Only a moment later the old man pushed Bob through the door.

"Bob!" Eileen barked.

"Who are you?"

"Do you have any medical training? Ethel tells me you're a healer."

"God, no. What the hell is going on here?"

"Help this girl," Eileen said fiercely as Bernadette wailed in raw terror.

"I've never done this," Bob said, ashen-faced. He knelt beside Bernadette. "It's okay," he said. "It's going to be okay."

"Great! Some fucking amateur is going to deliver my baby."

"Shush, Bernadette. He's all we've got. Can I get you anything?"

Bob's mind cast around wildly. "Towels. It's getting sort of messy here. Uhh . . . scissors? Some string? It's going to be all right, Bernadette."

"It's coming, it's coming," she gasped, then bore down hugely, emitting a primal roar. She felt as if she were almost physically coming apart, her body unhinged. A huge dark head slowly pushed out between her legs. At that moment Willie Peck stuck her head in the tent door. "Is everything all right in here? I thought I heard . . . oh dear."

"Stand back," said Eileen.

And as if it knew how to happen, the baby slithered out, a big fat red boy covered with white slime. Bob caught him in his hands and held him aloft. "He looks fine," he said, his face flushed with exhilaration. "Bernadette, you have a son."

"But I didn't do anything, " she said, awestruck. Bob laid the squalling newborn on her stomach. "He looks disgusting," she said, but her voice was full of tenderness. "Hello, Donovan."

"Is that his name, then?" said Eileen, relieved it wasn't something outlandish. Just then Dr. Bliss strode in with his black bag.

"What's this?" he said to the small group in the tent. "Couldn't you wait?"

As this ordinary miracle unfolded in the beer tent and the boozy speeches droned on, the Horgie Days Squirrel gently collapsed in a sodden heap while the crowd cheered wildly. And at the fringes of Gribble Park, Min's mystery guest finally arrived in a white sedan and got out on the passenger side. It was an elderly gentleman with a goatee, immaculately dressed in a white suit and string tie. He strolled towards the bandshell, but stopped to approach a lone figure standing at the edge of the crowd.

"Dorothy," he said, politely but warmly.

Dot looked up, a little startled.

"Harland." She pulled out a cigarette and waited for him to light it for her. "It's been a long time."

"That it has, Dorothy," he said to her. "That it has."

Epilogue: THE WEDDING

A young voice, almost silvery in timbre, echoed through St. Andrew's United Church, three years to the day after the blessed event in Gribble Park.

"My lover spoke and said to me, 'Arise, my darling, my beautiful one, and come with me. See! The winter is past; the rains are over and gone. Flowers appear on the earth; the season of singing has come, the cooing of doves is heard in our land.'"

In three years Bernadette had blossomed into an auburn beauty, full of grace and poise. Quite a lady, Eileen thought, as she looked up at her standing behind the pulpit, reading from the big old leather-bound Bible.

Ninian Sanderson had insisted on something scriptural, and though the Song of Songs had always scandalized him, he finally relented. Eileen would never admit this to a soul, but she had first heard those voluptuous verses from Shelton's lips almost forty years ago. To her, they were a tribute to the unquenchable power of love.

Eileen felt a fierce pride in her daughter as her voice rang through the church, and something even stronger than that. She stood at the front of the church in a pale pink satin dress, Cormac Pedlow by her side, their hands intertwined. When she looked into his heathery grey-green eyes, she felt a fire in her heart.

What amazed her is how sure she felt. After all those blunders, all those blind alleys and disasters, she was ready to try again. And Ninian went along with it! She'd been afraid she would have to go Episcopalian or even Unitarian to get married at all. Something must have happened to the man to soften his usual disapproval.

As Reverend Sanderson led them through their vows, Donovan Robert Connar squirmed in his pew, eager to get on with his third-birthday celebrations. It had been almost impossible to settle the dear little thing down enough to carry the ring down the aisle on a pillow (and even at that, he had managed to drop it three times). Then Eileen had followed on Aubrey's arm while Bertha McAdam played the wedding march from Lohengrin on the foot-pedal organ. Eileen insisted that this was to be a proper wedding with all the trimmings. And she was gratified to see that the church was full to overflowing. Forgiveness of her past sins? Or mere curiosity? It didn't matter. A full church was a full church, a blessing.

It seemed that Harman had broken out in weddings of late, even in the most unlikely places. This rash of nuptials had helped offset the melancholy of Min's passing at the age of ninety-two. There had been no theatrics, nothing at all to warn Aubrey that the time was indeed at hand. One night she simply stopped breathing.

And not one Connar in the whole connection had objected when Min left her entire estate in the hands of a sweet, little, black-haired boy named Donovan. He was to come into the possession of a quarter of a million dollars at the age of twenty-one.

Not long after that, Aubrey and Pearl Smith were

quietly married in a civil ceremony in Judge Randall's chambers. She moved into the old house without much fanfare and set to putting it in order. The place was pleasant again, cared-for, full of the smell of good cooking. She had given Buck to a yard sale where he fetched the handsome price of two dollars, and got rid of the ancient radio, which had suddenly shorted out and stopped working one night several years ago. "Good riddance to it," Aubrey said. "It never worked properly anyway."

But the most surprising wedding of all was the union of Agnes Flood and Charles Nutt, an elementary school teacher who had been a bachelor for forty years. Since Bob's sudden disappearance after the reunion, Agnes had carried on the spirit of his little group, holding a prayer and Bible study meeting every Thursday morning in Charles and Agnes's new home. Though the magic of those days would never be repeated, they still used Kahlil Gibran for their closing prayer.

All anyone knew about Shelton Gramercy was that he had moved to Toronto, borzoi and all, for reasons that no one could fathom. He mumbled something to Guy about a "mission," but no one knew what he meant. Even stranger was the trip Aubrey had taken to Edmonton several months after the reunion, "to see an old friend." He had been gone for three weeks, and came back so relaxed in himself that people wondered what it was about Edmonton that could so soften an old misery like Aubrey. He never showed the pictures of his new grandson to anybody, but kept them in a special place in his rolltop desk. Pearl knew about them, of course, but knew Aubrey well enough not to pry.

As Nin Sanderson pronounced the couple husband and wife, Eileen sent up a little prayer of gratitude. The two turned to face the congregation as Bertha broke into the triumphant chords of the Mendelssohn Wedding March. "Ladies and gentlemen, may I introduce Mr. and Mrs. Cormac Pedlow." As Eileen walked past the beaming, tearful crowd, the lush, vibrant words from the Song of Songs reverberated in her head:

"My lover is mine and I am his; he browses among the lilies. Until the day breaks and the shadows flee, turn, my lover, and be like a gazelle, or like a young stag on the rugged hills."

ACKNOWLEDGEMENTS

I wish to express my gratitude to my dear friend and "honourary sister" Margo Vandaelle for her support, encouragement and valuable comments, without which this book might never have been completed. Heartfelt thanks to my dear husband Bill for his patience and forbearance during several years of preoccupation with the project, and for his unfailing love and support. And all praise to Bohdan Siedleckie, a spiritual master masquerading as a violin teacher, for his role as mentor to my creative life.

Warm thanks are due to Ruth Linka, David Lloyd, Erin Creasey and all the good people at NeWest Press for giving me this opportunity, and Caterina Edwards, whose editorial wisdom, insight, encouragement and kindness made her a pleasure to work with. I am grateful to Linda Richards of *January Magazine* for believing I could do this, even when I doubted; David Middleton for the great photos; Jurgen Gothe for being a pal; Lorrane Brown, not just for all the helpful suggestions, but for her example; and my songwriting partner Bill Prouten for those three little words that mean so much: "You go, girl!"

I also thank the congregation of Eagle Ridge United Church, and in particular the Thursday morning prayer and Bible study group, my spiritual kin. And, I thank all of my beloved fellow travellers as we trudge the Road of Happy Destiny.

Margaret Gunning was born in Chatham, Ontario. Her broadly varied writing career began with the publication of a humour column in the *Hinton Parklander* in 1985. Since then she has published hundreds of articles in periodicals from Victoria to Montréal. Her poetry has been published in *blue buffalo*, *Room of One's Own*, *Prism International*, and *Capilano Review*. She has also published short-fiction and appeared on numerous radio and television programs. *Better than Life* is her first novel. She currently lives in Port Coquitlam, British Columbia.